TAFFY'S FOAL

Other Books By
ELISA BIALK

THE HORSE CALLED PETE

TAFFY'S FOAL

By ELISA BIALK

Illustrated by William Moyers

HOUGHTON MIFFLIN COMPANY · BOSTON

The Riverside Press Cambridge

The Riverside Press
CAMBRIDGE · MASSACHUSETTS
PRINTED IN THE U.S.A.

jB4722ta
Ref
cop.13

For

MY MOTHER

CONTENTS

TAFFY'S FOAL

I

Nancy and Taffy

NANCY Irwin pushed her small ten-year-old nose against the school bus window as it approached the farm where she lived with her grandmother. Sometimes she could see Taffy waiting at the fence, a bright caramel-colored spot against the November landscape. Today the horse was not there, and Nancy guessed that Timothy, the hired man, must have taken her into the stable.

The bus driver pulled to a stop, looked over his shoulder, and called out, "Here you are, Nancy." She was always his last passenger because she lived a greater distance from school than anyone else. Nancy sometimes wondered what he did with his time after he dropped her off and went home for the day.

What *did* people do when they didn't have a horse to ride, she asked herself as she got off the bus. Why, if she didn't have Taffy — It was silly even to think of such a thing. Taffy was everything to her!

Nancy took a short cut across the brownish grass to the kitchen door of the white farmhouse where she lived with Grannie. As she stepped into the kitchen, she could smell the coffee that was "perking" on the stove, and she knew that Grannie had company.

From the living room, Nancy could hear two voices — Grannie's and Mrs. Whipple's. Mrs. Whipple was a neighbor who lived up the road and liked to drop in about this time almost every afternoon. Nancy didn't care much for Mrs. Whipple. For one thing, she talked through her nose. Every word came out as if it was flattened first with a baseball bat.

Nancy wouldn't have minded Mrs. Whipple's unpleasant voice so much, except that what she had to say usually was unpleasant, too. Right now, for instance, she was saying as if she knew better than anybody else what she was talking about, "Well, after all, a horse is a horse — but a child's got to have other things too."

Grannie sighed. "I know."

"It'll be the best thing in the world for her. You've done your best, Agnes, but the child must certainly be lonely —"

Suddenly Grannie's voice cut in, loudly, "Nancy, is that you?"

Nancy came into the living room, kissed her grandmother, and greeted Mrs. Whipple. Besides the coffee, there was a plate of big homemade sugar cookies on the small table in front of the sofa.

"Here, dear," Grannie said, "help yourself."

Nancy took two. She loved those sugar cookies. As she bit into the crunchy goodness, letting the piece melt in her mouth, she noticed that Grannie wasn't in a dress this afternoon, but in riding clothes. She wore brown whipcord breeches and a white shirt, and she looked slim and almost girlish. Nancy thought of the picture hanging in the hall, showing Grannie as a beautiful young woman taking a high hurdle on a big white Irish jumper. Now Grannie's face, wrinkled like a butternut, showed that she had spent many years out-of-doors in all kinds of weather. But one could also tell, by her quick darting grace, that those years had been spent in good healthy exercise.

"Oh, you're going to ride with me today!" Nancy exclaimed. "Goody!"

"Yes, I thought I would," Grannie said. "Won't be many more clear days like this."

Mrs. Whipple didn't approve. She clucked over her coffee cup. "*I* gave up riding thirty years ago!"

"I don't ever intend to give it up," Grannie said briskly. "Not unless it gives *me* up first. Nancy, why don't you run up and change your clothes while I clear up these dishes?"

Nancy said good-bye to Mrs. Whipple and went upstairs, where she got into blue jeans, a T-shirt, and a leather jacket. She also put on her riding boots. She could wear her sturdy saddle-shoes if she wanted to, but the boots were a gift from her father and it was fun to wear them.

When she came down again, Mrs. Whipple was gone and Grannie was drying the dishes they had used. On the way to the kitchen Nancy stopped to look on the hall table, where Grannie always left any mail that might be of interest to her. She always looked for word from her father. He lived in Chicago, and his letters were the high-spot of the week. But today she didn't see anything on the hall table, so she came into the kitchen asking, "Didn't we get a letter from Daddy today?"

"Yes," Grannie said slowly, "we did."

"When is he coming down?" Nancy asked eagerly, as she always asked.

"He didn't mention it, though I imagine he'll be coming pretty soon." As Grannie put the cups and saucers away in the china cabinet, she added, "He's got something more important to tell us this time."

"*More* important than coming to see us?" Nancy scoffed. "It couldn't be!"

"Well, it is," Grannie said. She reached into her pocket. "I've got the letter right here — but I thought we might ride out to The Crest and read it together."

"That would be nice." The Crest was a place where they loved to go. Sometimes in the spring and summer they cooked their suppers there. Sometimes they just rode over to it when they wanted to talk. It was a beautiful spot, quite high over the land around it. It was the kind of place where people felt close to each other.

"Let's go!" Nancy cried, and hurried out while Grannie put on her jacket and an old felt hat. Over her shoulder, Nancy called, "I'll race you to the stable!"

Grannie laughed. "Don't you suppose I know better than to race with a spry ten-year-old?" But she knew Nancy couldn't wait to see Taffy, so she urged, "Run ahead, and I'll catch up to you."

Nancy ran across the familiar ground that led to the stable. She climbed a fence, and as she climbed she called out, "Taffy!" There was an answering whinny, and her heart gave a glad beat.

As she entered the stable she could see the horse's head sticking out above the half-door of the stall. She was a pretty horse, a smooth light tan, and her silky mane looked as creamy as the pulled taffy that gave her her name. "Hello, Taffy!" Nancy said softly. She put her arms around the horse's neck, and pushed her face down against the familiar warmth, and it seemed to her that she could feel love pouring out of her heart. Taffy in turn nuzzled her hair and her face and even one ear, which was left completely and stickily wet, but Nancy didn't mind at all.

As Nancy stood there she heard a sly chuckle in back of her. There was Timothy. He was a wiry man, lean and hard-muscled like so many men who spend their lives with horses. Nancy could never guess how old he was, but he seemed to have been here on the farm always. "You'd think you hadn't seen each other for six years, instead of six hours!" Timothy was saying.

"It always seems like six years!" Nancy answered.

Grannie joined them. "Have you saddled Blackie, Timothy?"

"Yes, Miz Irwin — I saddled Blackie. Like you said." From the tone of his voice, Nancy could tell that Timothy didn't approve of Grannie riding the big stallion. Blackie — whose registered name was Black Knight of Wales — was a high-spirited thoroughbred. And though Grannie had always been a wonderful rider, now she was — well, Nancy thought politely, not *quite* as young as she used to be.

"Now, don't you get to worrying," Grannie cautioned Timothy. "I can still handle a horse better than the next one!"

"Depends on who's the next one," Timothy muttered.

Grannie winked at Nancy, who always enjoyed the way she teased Timothy. "Trouble with having

6

help around for many years is that they always keep tab on your age." She mounted Blackie briskly.

Nancy trotted out on Taffy, leading the way. Blackie was really a faster horse, but Grannie held him in so that Nancy could set the pace. This was such a fast one that after a brisk canter Grannie called, "Nancy, let's take it a bit easier!" And she declared, panting, "Never thought I'd see the day when a child of ten could outride me!"

"*You* taught me how, that's why," Nancy called over her shoulder.

That made Grannie feel better about it. "Yes," she admitted proudly, "and I must say you've been a very apt pupil."

They reached The Crest, and dismounted. Nancy slid off Taffy and held Blackie's reins while Grannie got off, slowly. When she stood on the ground, Grannie rubbed a stiff knee and laughed, "Well — a person can fool himself, but he can't fool his bones! *Or* Timothy!"

Nancy touched her hand to Taffy's warm flank. "I hope I didn't ride *her* too hard. Is it all right to let her go fast now, Grannie? Even if she's going to have a foal?"

"May is a long way off," Grannie answered. "Taffy needs the exercise. When the time comes to slow down, you'll find she'll let you know."

Nancy patted Taffy fondly. "I wonder if she knows she's going to be a mother?"

"Why don't you ask her?" Grannie suggested with a smile.

Promptly, Nancy did. "Isn't it wonderful, Taffy? You're going to have a little foal of your very own. One that will look just like you. Or like Blackie. But I'd rather have it look like you."

Taffy pulled away from Nancy to graze at a patch of grass with Blackie. She shook her head, trying to free the reins from Nancy's hands. "What," Nancy exclaimed, "you don't *want* it to look like you? Why, Taffy, I'm surprised! A beautiful mare like you not wanting her baby to take after her!"

Grannie laughed. "Better let her go — the grass

is still greener here than anywhere else. And you come over here so that we can talk — we don't have much time left. It gets dark early these days, you know."

Nancy let Taffy go, and went over to sit next to Grannie on a large flat rock. From there, they could look across over the hills and meadows of Kentucky, and what they saw looked very good to them. The trees still wore their brilliant autumn dress, and the pines looked a dark bluish-green against all the color.

Nancy loved this scene. "It's nice to be here, Grannie, isn't it?"

"I've always loved it, too."

The feeling of being close to Grannie, of *knowing* her, settled down over Nancy with the late afternoon sunlight. "Grannie," she said soon, "what about Daddy's letter?"

Grannie brought it out. "Here it is, dear. Would you like to read it yourself?"

Nancy took it, but her heart sank when she saw that it was written by hand. When her father typed out his letters she could read almost every word without any help, but his handwriting was sometimes difficult. And this was one of the difficult times, because he seemed to have a lot to tell, and to be in a hurry to tell it.

"What does he *say*, Grannie?" Nancy cried in dismay after laboring through the first few lines.

9

"It all looks like little worms wriggling in different directions!"

Grannie shook her head sadly. "And to think that he once won a diploma for good handwriting!" Then she put her arm around Nancy's waist and drew her closer. "You know that nice young woman he brought down here over Labor Day?"

"Grace?" Nancy said eagerly. "Is he bringing her again?"

"Yes, I suppose he will, in a little while. But she'll be more than just Grace then, Nancy. They're going to be married soon."

"*Married?*" Nancy repeated. She remembered Grace as being tall, slim, pretty, and very nicely dressed, like a picture out of a magazine. Grace had been very sweet to her, and Nancy had liked her a lot. But to have her right in the family — well, that was something she simply had not thought about.

Grannie's arm tightened around her. "Of course I know it's a surprise," she said, reading Nancy's mind. "Everything is a surprise the first time you hear it. But you'll get used to the thought when it lives with you a little while."

"If — if Daddy marries her, then Grace will be like my mother, won't she?"

"She will be your mother."

"Well — not really."

"It's the same thing, Nancy. I think you're very

lucky — you and your father, both. Grace is a fine woman." Grannie laughed a little, in her special way. "And you know I'd be the last person in the world to say so, if it wasn't true!"

"But if — well, if Daddy marries Grace, will he still love us, too?"

"Why, bless you, he'll love us more than ever! People always have more love to give when they're happy themselves."

"Daddy has always seemed happy to me, Grannie."

"He's happy when he's *with* you. But he's been a lonely man since your mother died, Nancy." Grannie's arm tightened across Nancy's waist. "I'm very glad for him, dear. Now things will be different for him — and for you, too."

"For me?"

"Yes."

The single word whispered with the leaves still left in the trees. Suddenly Nancy knew that this was what Grannie and Mrs. Whipple had been talking about when she came home from school.

"Will I have to live with them, Grannie?"

"You won't *have* to, but I'm sure you'll want to. You'll have a real home there, with a father and a mother. And you'll be right in the heart of a big city where you can have lots of friends."

"I want to stay here with you, Grannie."

"You've always wanted to live with your father."

"Yes, but I wanted Daddy to come *here!*"

"It can't work out that way, Nancy. Chicago is where your father's furniture business is, and that's where he's got to be."

"And, of course," Nancy went on, "I never pictured him — well, being married."

Grannie had to smile. "He couldn't make a home for you, otherwise. A man can't take care of a child and an apartment all by himself."

Nancy pricked up her ears. "Apartment? Will we have an apartment?" She had never lived in one. As a matter of fact, she had never even known anyone who lived in one, although she often wished she did because she thought they would be such fun to visit.

"That's one of the wonderful things about all this," Grannie said. "They've found a perfectly beautiful apartment with a view of Lake Michigan. You see, they wanted to start right out making a home for the three of you together. Wasn't that thoughtful of them?"

"Yes," Nancy admitted, "it's very thoughtful. I appreciate it. But I'd still like to stay with you."

Grannie's hand patted her thick brown braids. "It's a change you'd have to make, sooner or later," Grannie told her softly. "Timothy's right, Nancy — I *am* getting awfully old!"

Nancy thought a minute. "It will be hard to leave — everything."

"Yes, it may be a little hard," Grannie said, "but you'll learn that nobody ever really leaves anything, or anyone, dear to him."

"You mean, I'll never forget you, or Taffy, or Timothy, or this Crest we love to come to?"

Grannie nodded. "And the farmhouse, and the stable, and the smell of fresh sugar cookies. And what it's like to wake up early in the morning and lie there pretending to be asleep, listening to the birds singing —"

"How do you know I do that, Grannie?"

Grannie laughed, and kissed the top of her head. "Because I was a child once, too. Oh, it was a long, long time ago — but I remember. It's like a picture carried in your mind. And that's what *you'll* do, Nancy — carry pictures along with you when you go to Chicago. Pictures of all of us here that you love, and all of the places that you love. Why, we'll be with you forever!"

Nancy put her hand in Grannie's, and let it stay there for a minute. Then Grannie said, "Goodness, look at that sun going down! We had better start back!"

They got to their feet, and Nancy held the reins while Grannie slowly mounted Blackie. Then she got up on Taffy. As she patted her mare's neck, Nancy asked the question she had put off asking:

"What about Taffy, Grannie? Will I be able to take her along with me to Chicago?"

13

Grannie said gently, "You'll be living in an apartment in the heart of the city, Nancy. There won't be any place to keep a horse."

"Is that what Daddy said in his letter?"

"Yes. He said he was afraid you'd feel badly about leaving her and that he wished there would be some way to take her along — but keeping a horse in Chicago simply isn't practical."

Nancy swallowed hard. She couldn't speak at all for a minute, and then she said, "We — we won't let him know how hard it *will* be to leave Taffy, will we, Grannie?"

"No," Grannie said softly, "we won't let him know. And you won't have to worry, because we'll take good care of her."

"I know you will, Grannie. Only — it will seem so strange to be without her."

"You'll have a lot of other things to think about," Grannie reminded her. "Moving to a big city like Chicago, and living in an apartment with a view of Lake Michigan, and everything."

"It does sound exciting, but —" Nancy murmured.

"And I think you'll be very happy, too, dear."

"Oh, yes," Nancy agreed, but the words didn't ring true. So she added half to herself, as they started down the hill, "At least when I get used to it, maybe I will."

2

"Meet Your Mother"

So Nancy's father and Grace were married quietly in Chicago, and started to live in the apartment they had furnished with such pride and delight. They wrote full details about every room except one. That was to be Nancy's, and a surprise.

Grannie sent them her lovely old silver service as a wedding present. It had been so much a part of the buffet in the Kentucky house that it might have been built-in. Every time Nancy walked through the dining room now, she looked twice at that blank space where it had stood, feeling as if there was a big hole in the room.

She made them a wedding present herself, in shop-work at school: a cute breadboard, cut to the pattern of a small pig. It had taken long hours of work for the cutting and sanding and shellacking. Nancy didn't mind the time it took, because she was putting not only time but love into it. But when she was

15

ready to send it, she didn't know how to address Grace. Somehow, she didn't feel right about saying, "Dear Mother." When Grace had visited them over Labor Day, she had asked Nancy to call her by her first name. That's what she finally decided to do now, simply starting her note with: "Dear Grace."

It was agreed that Nancy would stay in Kentucky until Christmas vacation, which would be a good time to break the school year. This would also give her a chance to have the holidays with Grannie before going to Chicago. Her father and Grace would come down for Christmas and stay for the holiday week, then take her back to their new home with them.

In the meantime, each day of these last few weeks seemed to fly faster than the one before it. Then the Saturday came when Grannie said, "I think we had better go out and look for our Christmas tree."

"Already?" Nancy said.

"Already?" Grannie repeated with a laugh. "Look at the calendar, child!"

They set out after the chores were done, so that Timothy could come along with them. Grannie always liked to pick out her own Christmas tree and have Timothy cut it down. To her, going to town and buying one took away some of the fun of Christmas. "Why," she would say, "I'd just as soon buy the fruit cake and plum pudding!"

Once that fall when she was riding Taffy, Nancy

had seen a tree which she thought Grannie would like. It was a pretty shape and thick through the middle. Now she led her to it, and Grannie said, "Yes, this is certainly a lovely tree!" Nancy was pleased, because Grannie was awfully particular about her Christmas trees!

"Too bad you couldn't find one closer to home!" Timothy complained as he chopped it down.

"Nonsense!" Grannie defended. "The prettiest ones are always the farthest away. I should think you'd know that by this time!"

"They seem to get farther every year," Timothy said as he huffed and puffed while chopping.

"It only seems that way," Grannie comforted. "But don't worry, we'll help you."

"Don't need any help!" Timothy answered indignantly.

Nancy helped Timothy, anyhow. Even Grannie lent a hand now and again, pretending she was only protecting branches as they went over rough ground. When they got the tree home, they stood it up on the back porch, a proud sentinel announcing that Christmas was almost here.

Nancy didn't need the tree on the porch to remind her, though. Suddenly she was caught up in the hubbub of excitement that went along with Christmas. Every day when she came home from school, the kitchen smelled sweetly of the rich cookies Grannie was baking. Grannie always left a piece of dough for her, so that she could roll out a few cookies and bake them herself.

They had other things to do, too. "How about the popcorn balls for the tree this year?" Grannie asked when they were finishing the cookies. "Think you'll still want them?"

"Oh, yes! The tree wouldn't look like *our* tree, without them!" And after all, this was going to be a very special Christmas. It was the first one Grace would spend with them.

They made the popcorn balls and Nancy had the fun of licking the sweet sticky syrup from the pan after the job was done. She also made the ornaments out of colored paper which she liked to hang on the trees, things like lanterns, and Santa Claus faces with cotton beards.

Some of the best fun was yet to come. Grannie beat up a special batch of gingerbread for the tree, and Nancy cut her own patterns for houses, and men, and a cat with a thick curling tail, and a Scottie with pointed ears. She always was sure to save enough dough for a very special piece for the tree: a horse. On this one, she pasted a bright gold cellophane mane, for Taffy.

Then it was the last day of school before the holidays, and Nancy suddenly realized how close the time was for going away. After New Year's, when she would go back to school, it would be to a new one her father and Grace had chosen in Chicago.

It was odd that all the time she had been going to the little school at the crossroads, Nancy had never thought much about the girls and boys who went there with her. She knew them, yes. And, of course, she talked to them during the day, and played games with them at recess and when lunch was over. But she never thought much about them otherwise, because when school was over they all went separate ways. They all lived so far apart in the country.

Today the boys and girls looked different to her. Kind of special, as if they all stood up one by one for her attention. Her best friend was a neighbor, Jimmy Bradford, who had gone away to boarding school last year. But now she realized that these children were really her friends, too, and it seemed funny to be leaving them.

Miss Kearns, her teacher, was pretty and young and Nancy loved her. She loved her even more this morning when she said, "You know, children, we're going to have more than a Christmas party today! We're also going to have a farewell party for Nancy!" Knowing that this was her special party made it a lot of extra fun.

Everyone had brought a little gift for Miss Kearns, but before she started opening her presents she brought out a box tied with a big red ribbon. "Nancy," she smiled, "this is for you."

"For *me?*"

"Yes. It's our way of telling you that we've enjoyed having you with us, and that we hope you'll be happy in your new school."

"Oh, thank you, Miss Kearns!"

"Open it up!" the other children were shouting. Nancy didn't need to be urged. Her fingers were already busy untying that big red ribbon. She took up the lid. Inside there was a shiny black patent-leather pocketbook, with a pretty new handkerchief, and a tiny address book and pencil in it.

All the girls said, "Oh, how pretty!" and the boys made silly remarks, as boys will. Nancy too said, "Oh, how pretty!" Then she closed the box and put it on top of all of her school things. She would never be able to tell Miss Kearns how much the gift meant to her, but she knew that she would want to keep it always.

When the party was over and everyone was going home for the holidays, Nancy was glad that she could say "Merry Christmas" to all of them. She thought that was much nicer than having to say "Good-bye." Each child had written his name and address in the little address book in her new pocketbook, and she promised to send each one a picture post card from Chicago.

"How lucky you are!" they all said. One girl said, "See the Natural History Museum for me!" and a boy said, "*I'd* want to see that coal mine I've heard about! It's in the Museum of Science and Industry."

Nancy promised, "I'll see them all!" She tried to make little notes alongside the addresses, reminding herself what each girl or boy was interested in, so that she could write about it on her cards.

But when she came home at noon, after the party was over, she was very quiet. Grannie, after admiring the present, put it back in the box and said: "We'd better wrap up our own gifts, or your father and Grace will be here before we're ready. The early train will bring them here about four o'clock."

"Then we'd better hurry, hadn't we?"

They brought out the gifts they had for Nancy's father and for Grace. Nancy used her prettiest wrappings for Grace's present — a handkerchief bought with her own money — because she wanted it to look especially nice. "How does it look, Grannie?" she asked anxiously.

"Lovely, dear. Grace will be so pleased!"

"I wonder if she'll like having Christmas with us?"

"I think so. She doesn't have any family of her own, you know. Except us now."

"I hope — do you think she really likes me, Grannie?"

"She more than likes you. She loves you already."

"How do you know?"

"You can't fool a grandmother."

"Grannie —"

"Yes?"

"Will you miss me after I leave?"

"Hand me that wrapping paper, please. No, the one with the pine cones on it. Thank you, dear."

"But will you, Grannie?"

Grannie hesitated a moment, and then she said: "Old people don't get lonesome, Nancy. They have too many things to think about — and to remember."

"But Grannie, I'm afraid I'll —"

Then Grannie did something she *never* did — she interrupted Nancy. "Got everything wrapped?" she asked. "Even Timothy's?"

"Yes. Even yours, in case you're wondering. But don't try to find it because you'd never guess where I put it!"

"I'm sure I wouldn't!" Grannie agreed. "As long as you're all caught up, why don't you have a little ride on Taffy?"

"What if Daddy comes?"

"I said a 'little' ride!"

"All right, Grannie." Nancy eagerly flew upstairs, into her riding things, and out to the stable.

Today, Taffy answered her touch on the reins almost as if she guessed what Nancy was thinking, without being told. It's just like being a part of her, Nancy thought. Then she wished the thought had not come to her. She *did* feel like a part of Taffy, and she didn't want to. Not when she had to leave her, and so soon.

Nancy rode to The Crest, and she dismounted for a few minutes to rest and look about a little. She could see patches of snow here and there on the hills, but there wasn't an all-over covering. Sometimes snow came very late in Kentucky, and some winters there was hardly any. Certainly there were no big blizzards such as her father said they had in Chicago.

Nancy knew that Taffy wouldn't like the cold winters around Chicago. She was delicate, and probably couldn't stand that sort of a climate. Why, here when a crust of ice formed over the wet leaves on the ground, Taffy showed quickly how she disliked it when her hooves crunched through as if they were breaking glass. No, Nancy said to herself, Chicago was no place for a mare like Taffy, even if they could find a home for her. Only she couldn't help wishing and wishing that she didn't have to leave her behind!

When Nancy got back to the stable, Timothy met her with a grin, and said as he took the reins, "Somebody's been out here looking for you!"

"Daddy!" she cried. She jumped down, gave Taffy a final pat, and ran to the house.

The minute she opened the door she could tell her father was there. She could hear his deep, booming, happy-sounding voice. She ran in, shouting, "Daddy!"

He met her more than halfway, a big, handsome man with dark curly hair and a wonderful wide smile. He picked her up by the waist as easily as if she were the size of a peanut. And he gave her a good hug and a kiss before he put her down again. Seeing him close-up like that, Nancy was surprised to notice how much younger he looked than he had the last time. And how much happier!

That reminded her quickly of Grace. She looked around and saw that Grace was standing at the door to the hall, smiling and waiting her turn. Remembering her manners, Nancy left her father's side, and said shyly, "Hello, Grace."

"Grace?" her father repeated heartily. "Is that what you're going to call her?" He put an arm around Grace, and an arm around Nancy, and he said: "Meet your mother!"

Grace laughed a little, easily. She put her arms around Nancy, stooped to hug her, and said, "Of course she'll call me Grace! Why, what would she call me? *Aunt* Grace or something?"

Nancy, grateful for this moment of quick understanding, pressed her cheek against Grace's cheek. It felt soft, and nice, and *good*. But it still felt strange.

3

Good-bye — and Hello

CHRISTMAS was a wonderful day.

Nancy jumped out of bed at dawn. She shut the window of her room against the cold, crisp air, and wrapped herself in her flannel robe and got into her felt slippers. Then she ran out into the hall, calling, "Merry Christmas, Daddy! Merry Christmas, Grannie! Merry Christmas, Grace!"

One by one they sleepily joined her in the hall for the procession downstairs. Her father turned on all the lights first because it was still very dark. Then Nancy raced into the living room to look, in wonder again as she did each year, at the big, heavily-trimmed tree, and all the gifts piled beneath it.

Grannie was always telling Nancy's father that he must not give her too much at Christmastime, that a child could only play with a few things at a time. He tried hard to follow her instructions, but of course he always managed to get in a few extras, as fathers will. This year the "extras" were swelled by Grace's gifts. She gave her a pretty red wool dress with bright stitching down the front, and a lovely small doll.

"It's for your collection," she said as Nancy opened the box.

"Oh, thank you!" Nancy said politely, because Grannie had brought her up nicely. She didn't tell Grace that she didn't have a doll collection. Somehow, dolls had never seemed important to her. There always seemed so much more to do out-of-doors than indoors. But she didn't want Grace to know that.

After all the gifts were opened they sat down to breakfast. It seemed nice that there were four now instead of three; there was someone to sit at each side of the table. Grace seemed to feel perfectly at home here, and she chatted brightly and made little jokes. Why, she's *fun!* Nancy thought, and felt easier about going to live with her.

They had all gone to Christmas Eve service in Louisville the night before, so they had more time to themselves this morning. They needed it, too, because this was going to be a busy day. Grannie always loved having a huge old-fashioned Christmas dinner, and today they were having extra guests — the three Bradfords. It was Jimmy Bradford who was Nancy's best friend, and Jimmy's father was *her* father's best friend. Naturally, they wanted the

Bradfords to meet Grace, and they were sure that Jimmy's mother and Grace would be the best of friends too.

While Nancy and Grace lent a hand with the cooking, Nancy's father helped, too. In all the happy confusion of Christmas Eve, they hadn't got around to decorating the living room and hall. Now he tied pine branches along the stair rail to the second floor, and festooned the mantel over the fireplace in the living room. Grace put on the big red satin bows that trimmed off the festoons. She did a beautiful job because she was an expert; she was an interior decorator by profession.

Timothy arrived in time to help with the finishing touches. Grannie always insisted that he join them for Christmas dinner, because she said he had been with them so long that he too was "family." Next the Bradfords came, jingling sleighbells to make a merry noise. Nancy ran out to the porch to meet them. She was eager to greet Jimmy, whom she had not seen since the Thanksgiving vacation when he was home from boarding school.

Jimmy said, "Catch!" and tossed a prettily wrapped Christmas box at her. Nancy could hardly wait until she got into the house to open it. But she waited politely, and gave him his present first — a catcher's mitt. When she opened her own gift she found a bronze model of a horse.

"How wonderful!" she cried. "It looks like Juniper." Juniper was the Bradfords' race horse.

"That's what I thought, too," Jimmy agreed.

"He shopped and shopped!" Mrs. Bradford laughed. "He wanted to be sure to find exactly the right thing."

"I did not!" Jimmy denied hotly, feeling a little foolish. "I just didn't want to buy anything sissy, that's all!"

All three Bradfords liked Grace at once, and she in turn felt at home with them from the very first because Nancy's father had told her so much about them. Dinner was a very happy meal. Nancy's father carved the huge turkey, and everyone tried to eat at least a small portion of everything that Grannie had put on the table. They all said they couldn't possibly eat any dessert, but they managed to get down a helping of plum pudding, anyhow. Grannie saw to that.

Later Jimmy and Nancy played with the big game her father had given her. He always included among her presents something boys liked to play with too, because he remembered what it was like when he was a little boy and went to visit girls who had nothing but dolls. So this game was just the thing to keep the two youngsters occupied under the tree during the happy Christmas twilight, while the grownups talked — mostly about horses, which the Bradfords raised. Before parting, they made plans to get together at the Bradfords' before Nancy would go up to Chicago. This made her realize how little time there was left here — time with Grannie, and Timothy, and Taffy.

The day after Christmas, she was in her old clothes early, and out at the stable. Her father and Grace and Grannie joined her there later.

Nancy's father seemed to understand about Taffy even though she didn't mention anything about the horse at all. "I wish," he told her, "there would be some way we could take Taffy along with us. But you know that's impossible, when people live in the city as we do."

"Yes, I know," Nancy agreed quietly, remembering that she wasn't going to let him know how much she hated to leave Taffy behind.

"And what's this I hear about her having a foal?"

"Yes — in May."

"It seemed like a good idea," Timothy defended. "If Taffy has a good foal by Blackie, why, maybe we could even start up a racing strain again."

Nancy's father shook his head doubtfully. "It *sounds* good — but we're not geared for raising thoroughbreds any more. Now it's just a farm."

"*Just* a farm!" Grannie repeated. She didn't like anyone to speak in that kind of tone about this land she loved so well.

"My father used to raise thoroughbreds, you know,"

Nancy's father explained to Grace. "Blackie here is the last one of them. His sire was a great race horse."

Grace gave Nancy and Timothy a sympathetic glance. "Well, perhaps it *would* be possible to keep the strain going."

Nancy's father answered gravely, "But I'm not sure we could do it, through Taffy."

This time it was Nancy's turn to explain to Grace: "Daddy never liked Taffy. He wanted to buy another horse for me, but I fell in love with Taffy the minute I saw her, and didn't want the other one."

"Yes," her father agreed, "it was a case of love at first sight — both ways. But I do like Taffy," he corrected. "Who could help it? I never knew a mare with a sweeter disposition. It's just that she's not the best thoroughbred in the world."

At this point Grannie added: "You see, Grace, the best thoroughbreds are a healthy lot, and Taffy's not very strong. Too much exposure, or bad water, or food not agreeing, and she's down with fever or colic or something."

"It's not as bad as that!" Nancy defended. "Why, she hasn't had a sick day for nearly three months!"

"That's a record, all right!" her father grinned. "Well, let's hope it's a case of prepotency, then. On Blackie's side, of course."

Grace drew her eyebrows together in a puzzled line. "Prepotency?"

"That's when a foal 'takes after' one of its parents," Nancy explained gravely.

"Oh! I'm learning about horses!"

Nancy's father grinned again. "In this family, you'll have to!"

Nancy begged, "Daddy, you'll let me come down for the foaling, won't you?"

"I will if I can. We'll have to see." He frowned. "Now, you're not going to keep on worrying about Taffy and her foal, up there in Chicago, are you?"

"Oh, no!" Nancy promised. She was going to remember those two words often in the next few months, and to squirm at the remembrance.

Never had she known a week to pass so quickly. It seemed like no time at all before her father said at breakfast: "Well, tomorrow we'll be eating breakfast in Chicago. Wait till you see that room Grace has fixed up for you, Nancy!"

"I can hardly wait!" she said, trying to sound pleased and excited.

"Want to have a ride?" he asked casually later.

"Yes," she answered, keeping her voice natural too. She knew this would be the last ride on Taffy she would have for quite awhile.

They made it a long one. With her father on Blackie, Nancy had to do some good riding to keep up. Even so she could tell that he was holding Blackie

in. "I'll never be as good a rider as you, Daddy!"
she wailed.

"You still have quite a few years to go," he grinned.
"Besides, Blackie's a faster horse."

"Do you ever ride in Chicago, Daddy?"

"Well — I haven't so far. Here a horse is a means
of getting around. You certainly can't call it that
in a city! And I don't care much about fancy riding
along the bridle paths on Sundays." Then he looked
at her, added kindly, "But I'll take you riding whenever you want to go."

"Thanks, Daddy, but I don't think I'll want to.
There'll be so many other things to do." Actually,
she couldn't imagine herself riding any other horse
but Taffy.

They raced back to the stable. Her father dismounted, and left her alone with her horse. Nancy
slid down from Taffy's back and pushed her face
against the mare's soft neck, and she patted her with
long strokes. The time had come to say good-bye,
but she couldn't say the word. "Taffy," she began,
and then she waited so long that the mare snorted
in her ear and made her jump. It made her laugh,
too. "Now, please," Nancy said, "remember your
manners!"

Again Nancy put her face close to Taffy's, and
her brown eyes looked right into the mare's great

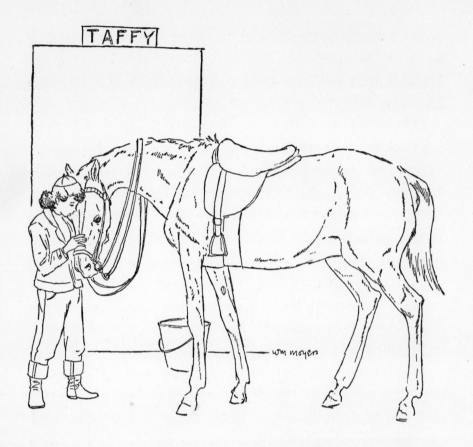

soft ones. It was easy to believe that Taffy was listening very hard. "Taffy," Nancy started again, "I've got to say —" She ended in a burst of words, saying something quite different from what she had intended saying, "Oh, Taffy, I do love you!"

Then she gave Taffy a quick pat, and turned away, and ran out of the stable.

Her father was waiting for her outside. He didn't say anything after she joined him, and while they walked back to the house together. But before they went in he said softly, "I'm proud of you, Nancy. I know that it's not easy to say good-bye to an animal you love."

Nancy swallowed hard, but when she spoke she was proud too because her voice sounded natural, "I didn't say good-bye. Grannie says we never really part from anyone, or anything, we love."

"That's true," her father agreed. "Take the two of us, for example. We've had to live apart for years, but that didn't mean we loved each other less, did it?"

Nancy thought for a minute. "I think maybe we loved each other *more*."

"I think so, too," her father agreed.

The bags were packed and they were all ready to go. Timothy was going to drive them to the station at Louisville in the old family car. At the last minute Grannie decided she wouldn't go along. "You'd be too crowded, five people and all that baggage," she said. Because her father and Grace didn't argue with her, Nancy knew that they all felt it would be a little easier if they parted here at the house rather than at the railroad station.

"I won't say good-bye, Grannie," Nancy said as she put her arms around her neck and gave her a big hug.

"Of course, you won't say good-bye!" Grannie

agreed. "Why, we'll be talking on the telephone every week, and you'll be down here for a visit as soon as the weather gets nice." She turned to her son as she added, "Don't forget, Michael. You promised."

"I won't forget!" he grinned. "Well, Nancy, let's go."

They piled into the car and got to the station in good time. Timothy got out and helped unload the bags, and then he stood there looking at Nancy a minute, not knowing what to say. Finally he said to her father, "The place is sure going to be quiet!"

"She'll make up for it when she comes back!" her father laughed.

"Yes," Nancy added, "we'll come back to visit soon."

"You better," Timothy mumbled. "You just better." Then he tipped his old felt hat to Grace, and got back into the car for the drive back home alone.

The train was ready, and they went right on. Nancy had never been in a drawing-room before, and she loved it. If she hadn't seen it with her own eyes, she couldn't have imagined how anyone could fit three beds and a tiny private bathroom into such a little bit of space!

Dinner on the train turned out to be fun, too. When they came back to the drawing-room from the dining-car, they found that the beds had been made.

Nancy decided she was ready for sleep — especially when her father said she could have the upper bunk if she liked. Lulled by the rocking motion of the train, she fell asleep as snugly as if she were in a cradle, and when she woke up they were pulling into Chicago.

The train was full as trains always are at holiday time, but even so, Nancy wasn't prepared for the crowd she saw when she got off at the station. Except when it was Derby Day in Louisville, she had never seen so many people all in one place before. But her father held on to one of her arms firmly, and to one of Grace's arms, and he guided them expertly through the station and to the place where a sign said, "Taxis." What was more, he even managed to get a taxi for them. He helped the porter pile in the suitcases, and before Nancy could catch her breath, they were skimming along the street outside the station.

The taxi cut in and out of traffic until it turned north on Michigan Avenue. Nancy gaped at the skyscrapers, and at the high white Wrigley Building standing guard at the Chicago River, then at the shops and parkways and at Lake Michigan itself as they swept along the wide boulevard with its exciting lanes of swift traffic.

Then the driver made a turn and pulled up before a high apartment building. "Well, here we are!"

her father declared. The doorman helped carry the suitcases, and they went up in a small slow elevator to the sixth floor. Her father took a key out of his pocket and put it in the lock. He flung the door wide open, and pushed her in first, saying, "Welcome home!"

Nancy stepped in eagerly and looked around. It was beautiful, and everything fitted together smoothly, but after Grannie's sprawling old house, it seemed crowded. However, she murmured, "How lovely!"

"You haven't seen anything yet!" her father said. He took her by the hand and led her to one of the two bedrooms that opened off the hall. "Here's your room. What do you think of it?"

This time Nancy didn't have to murmur, "How lovely!" The words flew out of her throat of their own accord. She had never seen a prettier room. Everything was new and bright, and there was a wonderful desk that would be all her own. It was true that Grace was an interior decorator, but anyone who looked at this room could tell that not only talent but love went into the planning of it.

Nancy turned to her with a heartfelt, "Oh, Grace!"

Grace put an arm around her. "I'm glad you like it, dear. And look, have you seen the view of the lake from your window?"

Nancy moved with her to the window. There was Lake Michigan again, six floors below, across the boulevard and a wide strip of concrete pavement. The angry-looking gray waves dashed head-on against the piles, leaving broken driblets that slid down the ice-encrusted posts.

"Goodness," she cried, "how cold it looks!" She couldn't help shivering a little, just to look at it.

Her father laughed and tweaked one of her brown braids affectionately. "It *is* cold, Nannie! Nothing colder-looking than that lake in early January! But wait until July. You'll love it, then!"

Nancy could feel herself shivering again. July was a long way off. Why, Taffy would have her foal before July came! But she mustn't think about that, she said to herself. This was her home now, and she had to start getting used to it.

She turned away from the window and said quietly, "Shall I start unpacking, Grace?"

4

The Dark Forest

MONDAY was to be Nancy's first day in the new school. She was going to go to a private one, because the public school was too far away for a girl in a strange city. "Do you suppose I'll like it, Daddy?" she asked at breakfast.

He joked about it, as fathers do. "If you knew what it cost, you'd like it!"

Grace suggested, "Would you like to stay home for another day or two, until you know your way around a little better?"

Nancy's father said, "Didn't you say you had an appointment with Mrs. Williams at ten this morning?"

"Yes, but if Nancy wanted to stay home, I could break it."

"I don't think you'd better. She's an important client."

Nancy settled it by putting in quickly, "Oh, but

I *want* to go to school today, really I do!" She finished her breakfast quickly, to be ready.

After today, the school bus would come right by the door of the apartment building. But this morning, Grace wanted to take Nancy to school herself. Nancy appreciated this extra kindness. She was learning that she could look to Grace for such little kindnesses, and for understanding. Already she liked Grace very much. If only, she thought, she could get to *know* her, with that kind of knowing that comes of living closely with someone, and of being able to guess what they are thinking!

The Wesley Girls' School was an attractive red brick building with a hedge around it. It didn't look in the least like the school at the crossroads back in Kentucky. Nor did her new teacher, Miss Foley, look at all like Miss Kearns, who had been quite young and pretty. Miss Foley was — well, maybe not *old*, Nancy said to herself — but she certainly wasn't young and pretty.

The class seemed very different, too. Instead of a roomful of noisy children, there were just about a dozen girls. She met them one by one, and took the seat given to her. Then Grace left, and Nancy bent her head down busily over her desk because she suddenly felt too shy to look up and see all those new faces around her.

Miss Foley told Nancy she thought it would be

41

best for her to go right along with the group's stud-
ies until she had a chance to learn just where she
stood. The first lesson this morning was in Science. They were studying about volcanoes. Each
girl was asked to draw a picture of what she thought
a volcano looked like.

It was easy for Nancy because she had gone over
this back home at the beginning of the year. She
drew not only the outlines of a volcano, but she showed
in the diagram how the crater went right down the
center deep into the earth. She also showed the
different levels of lava.

Miss Foley was so pleased with the diagram that
she put it up on the bulletin board. "I want all of
you to see," she remarked, "what a girl who has just
entered the class can do!"

Nancy felt she ought to tell them that she had already studied about volcanoes, but her new shyness
made her tongue-tied. She noticed that the girl next
to her, a girl with curly blonde hair and blue eyes,
whom the others called Pat, made a face. Instantly
Nancy thought: *She doesn't like me!* The thought
made her uneasy.

Next there was Discussion Period. "Nancy," Miss
Foley said kindly, "we'd all like to know more about
you. This would be a good time to tell us. You
came from Louisville, Kentucky, didn't you? Were
you born there?"

Nancy managed to answer, "No, I was born in Chicago. But I don't remember it. You see, I went to live with my grandmother when my mother —"

She hesitated before saying, "mother died," and Miss Foley went on quickly, "Louisville is such an interesting city, isn't it?"

"Yes. It was the closest city to us. But we lived in the country."

"Oh! Well — I'm sure it was lovely there." Miss Foley tried again, working hard to draw Nancy out, and help her over her shyness. "And it's wonderful riding country, isn't it? Do you like to ride?"

"Oh, yes!" It popped out, quite unexpectedly: "I've got my own horse."

There was a silence. Nancy could see the girls looking at each other. Then Pat laughed a little and said: "I'll bet you have! And I've got my own automobile!"

Nancy could feel her cheeks burn. But the girl who sat in front of her, a plump dark girl with a pretty face — her name was Evie — said quickly: "She's just teasing!" She turned around to look at Nancy, smiling in a friendly fashion: "What's your horse's name?"

Nancy told her, "Taffy."

"That's a pretty name for a horse," Miss Foley said. "And Patricia, you *were* very rude."

"I apologize," Pat said glibly.

The day finally drew to an end, and Nancy went home in the school bus, and up in the elevator to the apartment where Grace was waiting for her. She helped with the marketing and dinner. At the last minute, her father called to say he wouldn't be home.

"The January furniture markets are being held," Grace explained to Nancy. "That's his business, and he's got to be there. We may not see much of him for a week or two. But," she added as Nancy's face fell, "we'll keep busy, anyhow. I want to show you the city."

"That will be nice," Nancy said politely.

"We'll start Saturday," Grace planned with enthusiasm. "I don't work on Saturdays, so we'll have the whole day. Would you like to go to the Museum of Natural History?"

Nancy remembered this was one of the places she especially wanted to see. "Oh, yes!" she exclaimed eagerly.

"Then we could have lunch at Marshall Field's, and go to a movie at one of the big theaters afterwards."

"It sounds exciting!"

"Perhaps," Grace suggested, "you'd like to ask one of the girls at school to join us."

Nancy thought at once of Evie, who had quickly come to her defense. But she was afraid she didn't know her well enough yet. So she decided, "No, I'd rather not."

"All right," Grace said, "we'll have a happy day."

When Saturday came along, Nancy was very glad they were going to be busy. It was just a week ago since they had left Kentucky, and she found that her thoughts were still there more than in Chicago. And Saturday had always been the day she had spent the most time with Taffy.

"Well, have a good time, girls!" Nancy's father said as he kissed them good-bye.

"Don't forget you're to meet us for lunch, if you can get away!" Grace reminded.

"I'll manage to get away, all right!" he promised. "I wouldn't miss a date with my two girls for anything in the world!"

As soon as the breakfast dishes were done and the beds made, Nancy and Grace started out. A bus that wound its way expertly through the Michigan Avenue traffic took them to another that skimmed along the Outer Drive to the Field Museum of Natural History. It was an enormous place, looking like pictures of the White House, and Nancy wondered how they would ever be able to see everything in it.

Grace explained that it wasn't possible to "do" all of it at one time. "Not without getting so tired that you wouldn't enjoy it," she pointed out. They started on the first floor. Nancy was excited over the dioramas — arrangements in showcases which

45

gave a vivid lifelike quality to the animals and birds. There was a winter scene that looked so real, it was exactly like looking out of the window into the park.

Next, they visited the Hall of Man, where they saw sculptures representing many races of mankind. Nancy was even more impressed when Grace told her that the sculptress, Malvina Hoffman, had journeyed to far-off corners of the world to "do" the subjects in their own native lands. She stared at the figure of a pigmy and thought how wonderful it must have been to see strange people like this, and to learn all about where, and how, they lived.

It didn't seem long before Grace looked at her watch and declared: "Goodness, it's almost time to meet your father! We'll have to go!"

"So soon?" Nancy wailed. "We haven't even been upstairs, yet!" She looked toward the inviting wide marble staircase. "What's up there, Grace?"

"Wonderful things — the Hall of Jewels, beautiful costumes from other lands, science exhibits, prehistoric animals, *everything*. But there is too much to be seen in one day. Let's save it for the next time."

"All right," Nancy agreed. "But we'll come back again sometime, won't we?" she asked.

"Oh, yes! Often!" Grace promised, pleased that Nancy had enjoyed it.

Before they left the big museum, Nancy bought cards for the friends back at school in Kentucky who had been especially interested in visiting it. She knew they would be thrilled that she had already been there herself.

Nancy's father was waiting for them when they got to the dining room at Marshall Field's, and she was proud when she saw him. He looked bigger and more handsome to her than any other man in the whole store. They had to wait in line for a table, but the time passed quickly as she told him about all the things she had seen at the museum. He listened just as gravely and politely as if he hadn't seen all of those things several times over, himself!

Nancy felt very important when they finally got a table and her father allowed her to write down her own order on the check the waitress placed before them. But his eyebrows drew together when he saw what she had written. "A *peanut butter* sandwich!" he all but bellowed. "Is *that* all you want, after waiting all that time in line?"

"But I *like* peanut butter sandwiches," Nancy protested meekly.

Grace laughed at Nancy's father. "*All* little girls like peanut butter sandwiches," she told him. "I did myself when I was Nancy's age."

Her father's charming smile returned. "Well, live and learn," he said. "With two of you against me, I know when I'm licked!"

He had to leave them as soon as lunch was over,

but Nancy and Grace were not in a hurry. They shopped around for awhile, and Nancy was convinced that Marshall Field's must be the biggest department store in the whole world. Then they went to a movie theater close by and she was sure *that* must be the biggest in the world. The rows of balconies seemed to march right up to the sky.

When they came out, it was dark, and all the lights were on in the shopping district and on Michigan Avenue. Nancy kept her face close to the bus window going home, so that she wouldn't miss anything.

Back at the apartment, Grace found that a large package had come during their absence. "I've been waiting for this!" she exclaimed as she picked it up. And she added mysteriously: "It's something special for you, Nancy!"

"For me?"

"Yes, something I had sent up out of storage. I thought you might like it."

Nancy followed Grace into the kitchen while she cut the rope on the carton. There was a lot of paper inside, and between the wadded paper, wrapped carefully in tissue, were about a dozen small dolls. They were dolls of all nations: a little Dutch doll, and one from China, and another from Alaska, and from other far-off lands. They were tiny, but beautifully made and dressed.

"This is the doll collection I had when I was a

little girl," Grace explained. "I thought you might enjoy them, yourself."

Nancy picked the dolls up one at a time and examined them carefully. They were interesting, and she could sense how excited Grace seemed to be about them, but she wondered at her excitement. To her, dolls had never been much fun — maybe because it's never much fun to play with dolls alone.

There never seemed to be another little girl close enough to play with. But she wanted Grace to feel she shared her pleasure, so she said, "Aren't they lovely?"

Grace helped carry them to Nancy's room, and together they installed them in neat rows in the built-in shelves that had, until now, been empty. She stepped back for a look when the job was done, and said in a pleased voice, "There, now! You can put the little doll I gave you for Christmas up there, too. And we can add to the collection from time to time, until the shelves are filled!"

"Yes, that'll be nice," Nancy agreed.

Grace left her, to get the simple dinner she had planned, since there would be just the two of them. Nancy looked at the dolls again, and then she went to the bookcase and took out a horse story she liked to read over and over again. She settled down with it in her pretty little chair. After awhile a slight noise attracted her attention. She looked up and saw that Grace was standing at the door, glancing from the dolls to Nancy and her book. She could tell by the look on Grace's face that she was disappointed, although she quickly covered up her feelings with a smile as she said "Dinner's ready, dear."

Grace was rather silent during the meal, and Nancy could guess what she must be thinking. She felt sorry, because she hadn't meant to hurt her. Finally she said, "Grace, you loved dolls when you were a little girl, didn't you?"

"Yes, I did," Grace admitted. "My doll collection meant everything to me. But children are different. . . . Now, *you* prefer horses, don't you, dear?"

Nancy looked across the table at her, and her glance didn't waver. "Yes, I do. But I love your dolls, too, Grace — because they're yours."

Grace said, "That's very sweet of you, and I appreciate it." She thought for a minute, and then added, "And I'm glad you spoke about it. It will help us to understand each other, if we talk things over."

Nancy said what she suddenly knew to be true, "I think we understand each other pretty well, already."

"I do, too. There's an old proverb that goes: *The heart of another is a dark forest.* But I don't believe it. I have my own idea."

"What's your idea?" asked Nancy. It was nice to be able to talk together like this, easily and freely, the way friends talk.

"I don't believe any heart can be a dark forest, when it's lighted by love."

Nancy felt a lump rise in her throat. She knew this was Grace's way of telling her that she loved her, not because she was her father's daughter, but for herself alone. Knowing this made her feel even

51

closer to Grace. It made her feel as if she *belonged* here in this apartment, though it was so different from Grannie's roomy, sprawling house.

All this Nancy knew and felt, but she was too shy to speak it. Still, when dinner was over she helped Grace carry the dishes into the kitchen, and stack them, and wash them, just as she used to help Grannie. She was beginning to feel at home.

5

Always Taffy!

NANCY knew that Miss Foley was trying hard to make her feel at home at school too, and that she was kind even though she looked strict. But she couldn't feel quite at ease with the girls in her room.

They seemed so different from the children in Kentucky. And somehow they seemed to know more than she did. Not especially in classwork, but about what was going on outside. Nancy had always lived in a small world of her own and had never paid much attention to anything else. With them, it seemed just the opposite.

Every Monday morning at Discussion Period, for instance, all the girls talked about what they had done over the week end, and they seemed to be interested in a good many things. What Nancy liked best to do was ride Taffy and now she didn't have her. So when she was called upon, she really couldn't think of anything to talk about. It made her feel stupid.

The girl who sat in front of her — Evie — continued to be friendly. The first time Nancy wore the bright red wool dress Grace had given her for Christmas, Evie said, "What a pretty dress!" and Nancy, pleased, said, "Thank you!" She was less shy with Evie after that, and asked her questions whenever she wasn't sure about something. Evie always helped her cheerfully.

Nancy came to feel that Evie was her friend, and it was a wonderfully comfortable feeling, like warming up before a hot fire after a long winter's ride. Having a friend there made her like school better. But she didn't know how to go about getting acquainted with the others. She hadn't been used to making after-school plans in Kentucky.

Finally Evie made the first move. "What do you do after school, Nancy?" she asked.

"Why, I go home and do the marketing with Grace, and help her with dinner —"

"Grace?"

"My stepmother."

"Oh! . . . Well, why don't you come skating with us? We all go to the pond around the corner, after school."

"*Ice*-skating?"

Evie laughed. "What kind *would* it be, in February?"

Nancy didn't know what to say. She wanted very much to go, but she didn't know how to skate. So she tried to make an excuse: "I don't have any skates."

"You can wear my last year's hockeys. I got figure-skates for Christmas."

"Well, all right!"

"Good! Tell your stepmother she can pick you up at the pond at four-thirty."

Nancy told her father and Grace about her plans at dinner. She saw that they looked at each other quickly. Then her father said, "That's fine, Nannie! Glad you're getting along so nicely with Evie. But can you skate?"

"I don't know. I've never tried."

Again she saw that her father and Grace looked at each other. "Why don't you let us take you down to the Skating Arena for a few lessons, first?" he suggested.

"Can you two skate?" Nancy asked, unbelievingly.

"Grace is a wonderful skater, and I started skating with her last year."

Nancy looked from one to the other. If her father had learned to skate, certainly she ought to be able to! "Oh, I think I'll be able to manage!" she said airily.

"Fine! That's the right spirit!" Grace approved. "You try it tomorrow. If you like it, we'll have to buy you your own skates."

55

In the coat-room the next morning, Evie showed her the extra pair of skates. They looked easy to use, and Nancy couldn't wait to put them on. After school, all the girls walked over to the pond in a group, Nancy staying close to Evie because she felt she was her friend.

"Of course," she said to Evie as she was getting into the skates in the warming-house, "I may be a little unsteady the first few minutes."

"Everybody is!" Evie said. "Are you ready?"

"Yes."

Nancy got up, and found that a funny thing had happened. Her ankles had turned to jelly. Instead of holding her up, they kept turning from one side to the other in the oddest sort of way. Evie saw her surprised look. She put a hand on her elbow. "You'll get used to it!" she promised. "Come on, I'll help you."

Even with Evie's help, the going was tough. The minute she got out on the ice, Nancy's skates slipped from under her and she sat down, hard. Getting to her feet again was an awkward, humiliating process. What was more, she didn't stay on her feet long. She found herself sitting on the ice more than she was standing on it. Poor Evie didn't get a chance to skate at all, but she was very sweet about it, and tried her best to be helpful.

The worst part of it was that all the other girls

seemed to be able to skate so well. Especially Pat.
It seemed that every time she had another spill, Pat
would whizz past, long blonde hair flying as she
played tag, raced with the other skaters, had fun —
and never fell once!

Finally it was time to go home, and they went

back to the warming-house to put on their shoes. Nancy's ankles ached. "I didn't think it would be so hard," she admitted.

She was talking to Evie, but Pat, sitting close by, said brightly: "*I* could skate when I was six! Everybody in Chicago can."

"Well," Nancy answered, "I could ride when I was six! Everyone in Kentucky can."

"Ride what?" Pat asked in her pert way. "A merry-go-round?"

Everyone in the warming-house laughed also. They were laughing at Pat's little joke, not at Nancy, but the laughter cut deeply.

At dinner, she put off the questions her father asked her about the afternoon, and Grace, with an understanding glance, changed the subject.

The next day at school Pat asked: "Going to skate again today?" She might have been trying to be friendly, but Nancy thought she was making fun of her. "No, I'm not!" she answered.

Because she was afraid of being laughed at again, Nancy kept herself out of a lot of winter fun. She was cut off from Evie's friendship too, because Evie enjoyed skating every day during the season. That meant they were together after school only once a week, when their Girl Scout Troop met.

Nancy loved Scout Day and looked forward to it all week. The troop leader was Mrs. Thomas, who was Evie's mother. She kept them busy with interesting activities. Besides, something special was always turning up. Nancy felt a little awkward at some of the things. She hadn't been a Brownie, in Kentucky, so that all of the Scouting program was new to her. She thought how wonderful it was that all these girls had been together for two years as Brownies and knew each other so well. It was a little hard to be the only new girl among them.

One day when she came home from school, there was a letter waiting for her, from Jimmy Bradford. He usually wrote about once a year — boys don't care much about letter-writing. Even when he did write, he never had much to say. This time he hardly filled one sheet of writing-paper. *"Dear Nancy,"* he said, and started right off by misspelling a word. *"Tymothy said to tell you Taffy's fine. I saw him in Louisville when I was home Sunday. I'm fine too how are you? Your freind James Bradford, J. R."*

"What's the J. R. for?" Nancy asked, puzzled, as she handed the letter to her father.

He gave a great hearty laugh. "That's supposed to be short for 'Junior,'" he explained. "In other words, your friend James Bradford is named after his father. But he should have done it like this," and he showed her how to write it properly.

"Oh!" Nancy said, feeling very superior. "Boys are rather stupid, aren't they?"

Her father's eyes twinkled. "Seems to me that's what we used to say about girls."

Nancy took the letter to her room and put it, opened, on top of her desk. It made Jimmy and Kentucky seem close to her. Then she realized this was why Jimmy had written the letter. He was away from home most of the year himself, and he knew what it meant to be lonesome. She wished she hadn't said boys were stupid, even jokingly.

She tried very hard not to show how much she missed Kentucky, and Grannie, and Taffy, but loneliness has a way of creeping out somehow. Although she was doing well in her school work, Miss Foley had the feeling that secretly something was bothering her. She was a bright child, with a lot of charm. Yet it was plain that she still felt apart from the other children, and that meant she wasn't used to her new life yet.

Miss Foley also noticed something else. Sometimes during classwork, Nancy's mind wandered. Miss Foley could tell just by looking at her that her mind was far away. And when her mind wandered, she "doodled" — drawing pictures in her notebook, instead of copying notes from the blackboard.

Now, Miss Foley knew that when you "doodle" you're really putting down pictures of what is lying in the back of your mind. In that case, it wasn't

hard to see what was in back of Nancy's mind: all of the pictures she "doodled" were of horses. Some of the horses were running, standing, or jumping.

Sometimes she drew only the head of a horse, with a light mane. It was plain to see something was bothering her and Miss Foley thought she knew what it was. She decided to write her father and ask him to drop in for a conference.

When he got the note, he waited until Nancy was in bed, then showed it to Grace. "I wonder if she's getting along all right?" he asked with a worried frown.

"She *seems* to be."

"Sometimes she looks — lonely."

"She never says anything about Kentucky, or Grannie — or Taffy."

"No, she wouldn't. Nancy never was the type to spill over if anything bothered her. She just kept it bottled up inside of her. Well, I'll go in and see what Miss Foley has to say." He looked down at the letter again. "I'll have to manage somehow to get away early in the afternoon."

"Do you want me to go?" Grace suggested helpfully.

"No, thanks. I feel I ought to handle this myself."

He managed to get away, all right, and went in for the conference when the appointed time came. He and Miss Foley had a nice chat to get acquainted a little first, and then she said, "Nancy is doing very well here, Mr. Irwin. And yet I have the feeling she could do much better."

"Yes?"

"I have the feeling that something is keeping her from spreading out, from being herself."

"Do you think she's unhappy here, Miss Foley?"

"No, I don't think she's *unhappy*. That's a strong word. But I think she hasn't quite found herself here yet. I think —"

"Yes?" Nancy's father prompted again.

"I think she spends much of her time daydreaming about something else."

"My guess would be that it's that horse of hers, Taffy."

Miss Foley smiled and reached for a sheaf of papers. "Your guess is a good one. Here's some of her classwork."

Nancy's father thumbed through them slowly. Every one had a picture of a horse drawn somewhere on it. Some of the papers were covered with pictures of horses, after she had carefully written out her assignments. In spite of himself, Nancy's father had to grin. Then he shook his head. "Taffy, always Taffy!"

"I think she misses that horse dreadfully, Mr. Irwin! It's almost as if she left a part of herself there in Kentucky."

"I know," he agreed. "I can see signs of it, myself." He thought about it a minute, then spoke again, "If there'd be some way of keeping the mare here, I'd bring her up."

"Have you thought of boarding her, at some stables, or out in the country?" Miss Foley suggested.

Nancy's father shook his head. "It just didn't seem practical."

"In the city, that's what people have to do," Miss Foley pointed out. "Of course," she said in afterthought, "it *is* an added expense."

"If it would make Nancy happier, I think we could manage."

"I don't think there's any doubt that it would make her happier. It would give her the *interest* she hasn't found here, yet."

Nancy's father thought about something else. "There's just one thing, though, Miss Foley. Taffy's going to have her first foal the middle of May. She's a rather delicate mare. There's always the chance that there might be trouble."

"Yes, you *have* to consider that."

"On the other hand," Nancy's father said, as if he were talking it over with himself, "if anything were to happen down there in Kentucky, Nancy might never forgive herself. If Taffy were up here, she'd know that she had kept an eye on the mare, herself."

"That's a good point."

"Well — I'll talk it over with Mrs. Irwin."

Miss Foley got to her feet. "I know you'll decide on the best course," she said, and held out her hand.

Nancy's father shook it, and smiled his nice smile.

"I think Nancy is lucky to be in your class. You're a very understanding and a very wise woman."

Miss Foley smiled too, and she didn't look at all strict, as Nancy sometimes thought her to be. "I'm glad you said *woman*, not teacher," she concluded.

He talked it over with Grace later that night. "Of course," he said, "there's the added expense." They were still buying extra things for the apartment, and putting money aside to build a home of their own in the suburbs, as well. The cost of boarding Taffy would have to be added to the budget. "We might have to do without that record player for a while. What do you think, Grace?"

"I think we should do it *by all means!*" Grace approved heartily. "Why, we don't need a record player nearly as much as Nancy needs Taffy!"

"It might mean more trouble for you. Trips out to the country and that sort of thing."

"I shan't mind that at all."

He placed his hand over hers, said gently, "And some people call you a *step*mother!"

Even Nancy? Grace wondered, but she quickly pushed the thought aside.

Next morning at breakfast, her father kept grinning at Nancy the way he did when he had a big secret. Finally he said, "Nannie, how would you like to have Taffy up here?"

She stared at him, her mouth a big round O. The

cereal spoon she had been holding rattled to the floor. "Oh, Daddy!" she cried, and she ran around the table and hugged him. "Do you mean it? Do you really mean it?"

"We've been thinking about it," he said cautiously.

"But how could we do it? Where would we keep her?"

"I have an idea. But let's wait till Sunday when we can look around a bit. Now, do you think you could finish your breakfast?"

"I'll try," she said, going back to her place. She took the fresh spoon Grace handed her, and started again. But though she finished everything that was set in front of her, she didn't know what she ate. She had never in all of her life felt so excited!

6

It's More Than An Idea

ON Sunday, Nancy could hardly wait to start "looking around" for a boarding stable as her father had promised. But first, she went to Sunday school while he and Grace went to church. Then they had dinner together, eating out as a special Sunday treat.

Nancy felt as if she would burst if she had to wait another minute before starting, but finally they got into the car and set out. Now her father told her what was in his mind. "I know of a riding stable just outside the city limits. Thought we'd check there first, and see what they have to say about boarding horses."

"*Boarding* horses!" Nancy exclaimed. "What a wonderful idea! I wish I had thought of that before!"

"So do I!" her father agreed. "Miss Foley suggested it, when we had our conference."

"She did! Why, how *nice* of her!"

The riding stable was a big and busy place. It was exciting just to be inside of one again, getting a whiff of the sweet heavy scent of hay and horses. Because there was so much ice and snow, people were riding indoors instead of outside, taking their horses round and round the big arena. Nancy watched the riders while they waited to talk to the manager.

"Too bad you didn't change into your riding clothes," her father said. "Maybe you'd like to ride one of those horses, yourself."

But Nancy said, "No, thanks, I don't believe I'd care to." Somehow, it would seem disloyal to her to get on another horse, and give it even a little of the love and attention she had always given Taffy.

When the manager wasn't busy, he came over to talk to them, and Nancy's father told him what he had in mind. "We don't board horses any more, ourselves," he said. "We can't even get enough

men to take care of the ones we keep for riding. But I can recommend a good farm."

Nancy's face lighted up, and her father said, "That sounds like the very thing we're looking for!"

The manager went on talking while he wrote down an address. "You'll find the Stacey place fine for horses. We send our own there once in a while, when they need a rest."

"Thanks a lot!" Nancy's father accepted the slip of paper with the address, and Nancy echoed, "Yes, thank you very much!"

They got back into the car and drove out to the farm. It was northwest of Chicago, not too far out to reach easily. Mr. Stacey was at home. He was a big, kind-looking man who looked out of place in his Sunday clothes.

"Yes," he said, "we board horses. Come on out and have a look at the place."

He got into his boots, and took them around the clean-looking barn and stable. His son, Paul, who was a big boy of fourteen, came along. "Is it *your* horse?" he said to Nancy. "Gosh, I didn't get a horse of my own until last year!"

"I was lucky," Nancy admitted.

"What's your horse look like?" Paul wanted to know.

"Oh, she's beautiful! Light tan and shiny and smooth, with a taffy-colored mane. That's why I call her Taffy."

"Sounds pretty, all right." Paul thought a minute, and then he said importantly, "I'll give her a lot of attention, myself."

"That will be wonderful!" Taffy was used to a lot of loving. Nancy knew that even if she wasn't at Grannie's now, Timothy gave it to her. It would help a lot to know that Paul would keep a special eye on her.

In the meantime Mr. Stacey and Nancy's father were talking things over. They came to suitable terms, and then the only thing that had to be settled was the question of when to move Taffy up from Kentucky.

"I wouldn't suggest moving her until the weather warms up a bit," Mr. Stacey said.

Nancy's heart sank, especially when she heard her father agree: "No, certainly not. I think we ought to wait until April."

She couldn't help cutting in with an anguished, "*April?*"

"Well, March, at best."

Nancy still looked downcast.

"Now, you wouldn't want Taffy to come up into weather like this, would you?" her father asked reasonably. "She's not used to this climate. Why, I'll bet your toes are tingling with cold right now."

"They are," she admitted.

"And Taffy can't wear snow-boots the way you can!"

Nancy laughed at that. "All right," she finally said, "we'll wait until March."

But now in February, March seemed a long way off. She didn't know how she could possibly wait for the month to go by. It seemed as if her father and Grace could guess how impatient she was because the next Sunday they had a surprise for her.

"We're going to take you down to the Skating Arena," they announced, "and teach you how to skate."

She wasn't sure whether or not she was pleased, remembering her one and only experience on the ice. "I don't think I can learn," she said in a humble voice.

Her father laughed. "With two of us holding you up, you can!"

Grace disappeared for a minute, and came back

with a box which she handed over with a pleased smile. Nancy could tell what it was by the weight. She wasn't surprised when she saw the white ice-skates inside it.

She didn't want them to think she didn't like the gift, so she said, "Oh, thank you!" And she pretended to be eager about going to the Arena.

As it happened, she had a wonderful time. It was true that there was a great difference between getting out on the ice alone for the first time, and having two good teachers like her father and Grace with her.

First, she skated between them until she got the feel of the ice under her and could keep her balance. Then she skated with one or the other. She was surprised to see how well her father could skate, since he had only learned the year before. But she was even more surprised to see what Grace could do. She was light as a feather on the ice, and did some fancy figures that even strangers watched admiringly. Nancy was proud of her.

"I wish I could skate as well as you can!" she said when Grace was giving her another lesson.

"Why, you'll be able to in no time at all!" Grace encouraged. "You've got good co-ordination, and that's what's important."

"What does that mean?" Nancy asked.

"Well, simply put, it's having all your muscles move at the same time."

Nancy took a few quick steps, to keep from falling. "And you think I've got it?" she asked doubtfully.

"I *know* you have! I've seen you ride Taffy, don't forget. If you have co-ordination in one sport, **you** will have it in another."

Thus encouraged, Nancy finally tried skating alone. She fell down a few times, but didn't do badly at all, for a beginner. And by the end of the afternoon she was doing very well.

"Would you like to skate again with the girls during the week?" Grace asked her on the way home.

Thinking of how she had kept falling down the first time she skated with them, Nancy had to laugh. "Yes, I would!" she said. "They'll be surprised!"

They were, too. Even Pat said, "Goodness, you learned fast!"

"I had two good teachers," Nancy said modestly. "My father and Grace."

"You lucky duck! I'd like to see *my* parents skating!"

Nancy skated every day after school for a week, and again at the Arena next Sunday with her parents. She was surprised how easy it was, once you caught the knack of it. And now that the skating season was practically over, she wished she hadn't missed those extra weeks of fun she might have had, if she hadn't been so afraid of being laughed at!

But now that the ice was going it meant that winter was just about over, and that Taffy could come up. Nancy could hardly wait to go to Louisville. She told Evie all about it, and they discussed the exciting plans. They were going to bring the mare up in a trailer attached to the car, and then ship the trailer back to the farm.

Pat overheard some of their conversation. "Will we get a chance to see Taffy when she gets here?" she asked eagerly.

"Oh, yes!" Nancy told her proudly. "You'll *all* get a chance!" Why, she could hardly wait to show Taffy off, because she thought she was the prettiest horse in all the world.

"It must be fun, being in Kentucky," Evie said.

"It is!" Nancy agreed. And she said in afterthought, "This time won't be quite so much fun, because the trip will be so short, and we'll have really only one day there. We'll have to start back early Sunday, you know. But sometime when we go down, would you like to come along?"

"Would I!" Evie squealed so loudly that Miss Foley rapped for attention.

The night finally came when her father said at dinner: "Well, this last thaw got rid of the snow pretty well. I think the worst of the cold weather is over."

"Oh, Daddy! That means Taffy can come up, doesn't it?"

"Yes, I think it's safe enough now. I've got things quite well taken care of down at the office, too. If it's all right with you girls, we can drive down to Louisville this week end."

"*All right!*" Nancy shouted. And to Grace she said, "Aren't fathers funny!"

Her father and Grace picked her up after school on Friday and started right out. "You'll have to sleep in the car part of the way," he warned her. "We won't get there until late tonight."

"I've slept in the car before," Nancy agreed cheerfully.

None of them talked much because her father kept his mind on driving, and she and Grace were busy with their own thoughts. The roads were clear, finally, and they made good time. Better time than they would make on the way back when the trailer with Taffy would be hitched on behind.

They stopped for dinner, then sped on again. "I don't hear you singing your theme song, Nancy!" her father teased.

"What theme song?" Nancy asked innocently from the back seat.

" 'My Old Kentucky Home!' "

"She doesn't have to sing it!" Grace laughed. "Everything she has said and done since she knew we were going, sang it for her!"

"You two girls get on pretty well, don't you?" he remarked fondly.

75

Grace replied lightly, "We seem to stand each other quite well!"

"Did you hear that, Nancy?" Her father was teasing again. "Think you can stand Grace pretty well?"

"*Stand* her!" Nancy cried. "Why, she's the nicest stepmother any girl ever had!"

Grace didn't say anything. Somehow she didn't seem pleased. Nancy wondered why. She had tried to make the best compliment she could think of.

Later, after dark, she fell asleep in the back seat, covered by a nice warm auto-robe. But it was as if she knew her way through the darkness in her sleep, because when they were a half hour out of Louisville, she woke up again, asking sleepily, "Almost there?"

"Almost."

Her father's single word was like magic. She pushed her feet to the floor and sat up, not sleepy at all any more. "Goodness," she said, as if she could hardly believe it, "in just a little while I'll see Taffy!"

"Not until morning!" he said in his now-I'm-being-firm voice, and Nancy agreed, "All right, but I'll be up early in the morning!"

She pinched herself to make sure she wasn't dreaming. Tonight she would see Grannie, who most certainly would be waiting up for them. And in the morning she'd see Taffy!

7

"My Old Kentucky Home"

NANCY *was* up early in the morning. She dressed quickly in her familiar blue jeans, T-shirt, boots, and leather jacket, and came downstairs. She had really hoped that she could sneak out to the stable before breakfast, but Grannie was up ahead of her.

At the bottom of the stairs, Nancy stopped and sniffed. Grannie was making pancakes! She realized this was one of the two fragrances that came to her whenever she thought of the rambling old house here. She could never remember it without thinking also of those wonderful pancakes and those sugar cookies she loved so well!

She quickly gave up the idea of going to the stable first, and hurried into the kitchen instead. There she kissed her grandmother's cheek and gave her another hug, almost as big a hug as she had given her last night when they drove in.

"Did you sleep well, dear?" Grannie asked.

"Oh, yes!"

"And you're not tired?"

"Not a bit! I slept part of the way in the car."

"Well, that's good. You were so excited when you came in, and you chattered so much, that I pictured you chattering all the way from Chicago!"

"That would be a long way to chatter."

"Not for you!" Grannie laughed. She piled a mound of tiny round pancakes on a plate and put it in front of Nancy on the fresh red and white checked tablecloth. "Better fill up!" she cautioned. "I thought we might cook our lunch out at The Crest if your father wanted to, and that means you won't eat again for some time."

"He'll want to, all right," Nancy promised. "Why, he wouldn't want to miss *that* for anything. And it will be a good way to show Grace our favorite spot."

"That's what I thought, too," Grannie smiled.

Nancy dug her way through the pancakes with her knife and fork. They were just as good as ever, which was saying a lot!

Between mouthfuls, she managed to ask, "Grannie, you don't mind that we're taking Taffy back with us, do you?"

"No, dear, I don't *mind* at all. She's your horse. But you'll find her a great responsibility."

"I know. That's what you've always said, that

a horse is a great responsibility. But I do so want her near me, Grannie!"

"Then it should be worth the time and effort," Grannie said quietly.

Someone else was coming down the stairs, and Nancy could tell by the light step that it was Grace and not her father. She came into the kitchen looking very pretty in a soft blue robe, and she called cheerfully, "Good morning, Mother! Good morning, Nancy! May I sit down here, too?"

"Oh, dear!" Grannie fussed. "I've set the best linen and silver for you and Michael in the dining room!"

Grace leaned over and kissed Grannie lightly on the cheek. "Goodness, are you going to treat me like company?" she teased. She pulled out a chair and sat next to Nancy. "Please let me eat right here!"

Grannie smiled and gave in. "It *is* cozy, isn't it?"

"It certainly is! And besides, Michael is still sleeping and isn't showing any sign of waking up!"

Grannie said with satisfaction, "Michael always sleeps late here. He makes fun of that old mattress — says it's like a hammock — but I'm sure he never rests better anywhere else."

Nancy and Grace both knew what he said about that mattress in private, that he would rather sleep on a board, but they kept their faces straight while Grace agreed tactfully, "I'm sure he doesn't."

"A mattress has got to be molded to a man's shape to be really comfortable," Grannie declared. "Otherwise, he might as well sleep on a board."

This time Nancy choked over the last bite of her pancakes. "Goodness, child," Grannie said innocently, "don't swallow your food without chewing!" To Grace she added, "I know she can't wait to see that horse of hers!" And again to Nancy, "Well, run along!"

Nancy didn't have to be coaxed. She was already halfway there, buttoning her jacket as she ran.

When Nancy was gone, Grannie turned from the stove to Grace, and her eyes were warm with sympathy. "You'll have your hands more than full, with the child *and* the horse!"

"Perhaps," Grace admitted. "But Mother, she *needs* Taffy!"

Grannie nodded so hard that one of the big heavy hairpins she used fell out and played hopscotch across the hot stovelid. "I know," she agreed. "But she will have to learn there are other things, too."

"I think she will learn," Grace said. "She just needs a little more time."

Nancy had a happy hour in the stable, with Taffy and Timothy, and then her father joined her. He looked Taffy over himself, and talked to Timothy about his plans for moving the mare up north. Timothy showed him the work he had done on the trailer to put it in good shape for the trip, and Nancy's father gave his hearty approval.

Then Nancy and her father saddled Taffy and Blackie and rode over to their neighbors, the Whipples. There they borrowed two more horses, so that all four of them — Nancy, her father, Grannie and Grace — could ride up to The Crest for a picnic lunch.

When they came back Grannie had everything ready, packed in four separate bundles, so that each could carry something and not load everything on one horse. She was used to packing like this for long horseback rides.

Grace was a little nervous because she didn't ride much, but she was a good sport and tried not to show it. Nancy's father had given her the Whipples' gentle strawberry roan, and after the first few minutes her confidence came back to her and she was riding it nicely. "If only," she sighed to Nancy, "I could ride like you!"

"You can," Nancy answered. "Remember what you told me when we went ice-skating the first time? You've got good co-ordination, too."

"But does the horse know it?" Grace asked, and they had a good laugh together.

Spring came early to Kentucky. In Chicago March was often bleak and drab, but around Louisville it was lovely. The grass was green, the spring flowers were up, and the hills were coming to life with a sudden rush of leafing trees. The air was soft and warm, too.

It was such a pleasure to be here on a lovely spring day like this, riding Taffy again, that Nancy was quiet for a full ten minutes. Twice her father had to look around to be sure she was still with them. "Are you feeling all right?" he finally joked, and she answered with a happy sigh, "Oh, Daddy, it's so nice to be back!"

They hadn't told Grace about The Crest, or what it meant to them. They wanted her to find out for herself. When they had climbed up to it, they all sat in the saddle for a little while, looking around over the beautiful view spreading out before them.

Then Grace said in a small voice, "Why, this is heavenly! No wonder you all love this spot!"

Nancy and her father looked at each other and smiled a satisfied smile. They would have been disappointed if Grace had not appreciated it. To them this proved she really belonged here, too!

Food always seemed to taste better to Nancy when it was eaten out-of-doors. Her father built a fire, and Grannie unpacked the four kits and spread everything out. She had arranged ground beef in flat patties at home, and wrapped each patty separately in waxed paper. Now she took them apart, unwrapped them, and carefully laid them in a hot skillet.

While they were simmering she unpacked a jar of potatoes which she had partly cooked and chopped up at home. Nancy watched her spread them in another hot skillet, and she cried out, "Oh, goody! Hash-brown potatoes!" They were her special favorites.

Grannie had also brought along olives and celery and carrot sticks, and some fresh brownies cut in generous squares. And of course there was fruit, because Grannie, having grown up in the country where vegetables and fruits were plentiful, felt that a meal was never complete without both.

Nancy ate a double portion of everything and wondered if she could possibly eat another bite. But

83

Grannie saw her looking thoughtfully at the fire that was still blazing brightly, and seemed to read her mind.

"Here," Grannie said, digging into a kit and bringing out a package of marshmallows, "there's no use letting that fire go to waste, is there?"

"That's just exactly what I was thinking!" Nancy said. She found a pronged stick and set to work, happily toasting marshmallows for everyone as they relaxed, there on The Crest, enjoying the beautiful view, while the horses feasted on the good sweet grass.

It was with an effort that they finally brought themselves to leave this favorite spot of theirs. But the day's pleasures were by no means over. After they had returned the horses to the Whipples, Nancy's father suddenly grinned at her and asked, "How would you like to take a ride over to the Bradfords? I hear Jimmy is home from school this week end."

The Bradfords were not only the parents of her good friend Jimmy, but they were also the owners of some wonderful horses — *and* the race-horse Juniper. Nancy's "Yes!" resounded all over the lovely Kentucky landscape.

Jimmy came running to meet them — he had been able to tell it was Nancy from the distance. "Gosh, Nancy," he beamed, "I'm glad you came over! I didn't know you were back!"

"It's only for a day," she said as she slipped off Taffy's back. "But it's wonderful to be here even that long!"

Her father and Jimmy's father were pumping each other's arms the way men do when they are glad to see each other.

"How's Juniper coming along?" her father asked. "We keep reading about him in the papers even in Chicago!"

"He's in fine shape," Jimmy's father said. "Want to see him?"

"What a question!" Nancy's father laughed.

Jimmy's father led them over to the low white building where the horses were kept. He was very proud of his fine thoroughbreds and took wonderful care of them. Nancy loved all the horses in the stable, but she loved Juniper best of all. He was a sleek black horse who looked a little like their own Blackie, but without white markings. He was black all over, and his eyes were wide and intelligent. And, of course, he was beautifully kept and curried. It was a joy to Nancy just to be able to look at him.

"He certainly looks good to me!" Nancy's father said after looking him over.

"It's what he does that looks good to me!" Jimmy's father grinned. "Look at this! Here's his time-record for the week!"

Nancy's father looked down at the sheet of paper,

85

and whistled. "Boy, it certainly looks as if you've got the winner this time!"

"That's what we hope!" Jimmy's father said with pride and pleasure. "Coming down for the Derby?"

"I don't know."

"You don't know! Why, you haven't missed a Derby as long as I can remember!"

"Oh, Daddy, do let's come!" Nancy begged.

"Sure!" Jimmy said. "Why, everybody's got to see the Derby!"

Nancy's father laughed. "*Everybody* doesn't, though. It just seems that way on Derby Day. But I'll see. We'll certainly come down if we can."

"Why, of course," Jimmy's father urged. "You'll have to help cheer for Juniper! In a big race, a horse needs all the help he can get!"

While their fathers talked, Jimmy showed Nancy a new colt. "Isn't he a beauty?" he boasted.

"He certainly is!" Nancy agreed. "I hope Taffy's foal will be as pretty! Jimmy," she said as an afterthought, "you don't think the trip to Chicago will be bad for Taffy, do you?"

"Gee, I don't know — but I shouldn't think so. Dad's moved all kinds of horses back and forth all over the country and it's never hurt any of them at all."

"But Taffy's kind of —" Nancy hesitated. She hated to say, "delicate" and tell about her fear, even to someone she knew as well as Jimmy.

Too soon it was time to go back to Grannie's. Nancy's father wanted to have everything in order for the trip home the next day, as he wished to get off to an early start.

Jimmy saddled his own horse and rode home with them so that he and Nancy could have a longer visit together. At her gate, he waved and said, "Well, so long — see you on Derby Day!"

Timothy was waiting at Grannie's, ready to lend a hand. He was so quiet that Nancy could tell he didn't approve of moving Taffy. On the other hand, he was so fond of Nancy that he didn't want to upset or discourage her, so he didn't say anything. She pretended she couldn't guess what was passing through his mind. In her own heart, Nancy felt *sure* that Taffy would come through everything all right, and she didn't want anyone else to have any other thought about it.

They hitched the trailer onto the auto, and packed all of Taffy's gear into the luggage compartment of the automobile. Right after dinner, they all turned in to get a good night's sleep. Bright and early the next morning, Taffy was led up a ramp into the trailer. Nancy's father covered the mare with a blanket, a light one which would keep off the cold breezes that might be felt as they drove north.

Nancy kissed Grannie and waved to Timothy.

"Good-bye," she said, "see you the first week end in May."

"The first week end in May?" Grace repeated, puzzled, as they started out.

"Yes — that's the Kentucky Derby."

"Oh! And are we really coming back for it?" Grace asked Nancy's father.

His grin spread straight across his face. "Do you suppose I'll be able to get out of it?" he asked.

Grace turned around to look at Nancy's eager face. "No," she smiled, "I don't suppose you will!"

"I should say not!" Nancy shouted.

She turned around to wave at Taffy, standing there in the trailer hitched to the back of their car. She couldn't swear to it, but it seemed to her that Taffy smiled back at her!

8

The Girl Scouts Meet Taffy

AS Grannie had said, a horse was a great responsibility. But Nancy was willing to accept the responsibility because she loved Taffy.

She found that having the mare close to her changed her life quite a lot. For instance, she didn't feel free any more to make week end plans with Evie or any of the other girls. Nor was there time, now, for those pleasant trips she used to have with Grace, when they would explore the different museums and parks and places of interest.

Because Taffy was near her, Nancy felt she wanted to spend all of her spare time with her. It was true that Mr. Stacey took good care of the mare, and that the farmer's son Paul gave her extra attention. Yet Nancy knew what it meant to be away from home, and she felt she owed it to the horse to be with her every minute that she could.

On Saturdays, Nancy went out to the Stacey farm and spent the whole day there. When her father could get away he drove her out. If he was busy, Grace was very sweet about taking Nancy herself. Sometimes she would ride one of the other horses while Nancy rode Taffy, even though she still didn't care much about riding.

Their Sundays followed the same pattern. After Sunday School and dinner, Nancy would change from her best clothes into her blue jeans and jacket, and off they would go to the farm. Sometimes during the week, when her father wasn't going to be home for dinner, Grace would drive her out for an extra visit, and they would have a simple supper together when they got back.

With this routine Nancy didn't have time for anything else. Yet all the girls asked her to be with them more than ever now, because she was herself again. She was the Nancy Irwin she used to be in Kentucky, relaxed, likable, and cheerful — the way she used to be with Jimmy.

Finally Nancy hit on a plan by which she could see her school friends, and still get to see Taffy too. She talked it over with Grace. "I know that all the girls would like to meet Taffy," she said. "Do you suppose there'd be some way that we could get the whole room out to the Stacey farm?"

Grace was enthusiastic. "That sounds like a good

idea! Suppose I talk to Miss Foley and see if she has any suggestions!"

Miss Foley was highly enthusiastic, too. "Nancy has blossomed out so much already!" she told Grace. "Giving the other girls a chance to see her with Taffy would be just the thing to bring her out completely." And she suggested, "Why don't you make it a Girl Scout project? Mrs. Thomas, the troop leader, is so wonderful at planning outings like that!"

So Grace got in touch with Mrs. Thomas. "Why, how grand!" the Scout leader exclaimed. "Evie has talked of nothing but Taffy ever since the horse came up here. By this time I can hardly wait to meet her myself — and I know all the Scouts feel the same way."

They discussed plans, and finally arranged a day when Grace would be able to get away earlier than usual. They invited another mother to drive also so that the cars wouldn't be too crowded. Miss Foley said the whole group could be dismissed an hour early, to give them more time at the farm, if they agreed to make the trip a Nature Study project. Of course, the girls said they would.

On the way out to the farm, they watched for the trees that were budding now that April was there, and made notes as they named the different kinds. Once they drew up to the side of the road when they saw a field of wild flowers. They picked a few anemones, blood-root and trillium, intending to show them to Miss Foley during Discussion Period the next day. Nancy happily discovered the last of a late-blooming dog-tooth violet patch. In Kentucky, this variety bloomed very early in the season. She was also able to name all the flowers the other girls found, and went on to the farm with the satisfied feeling that after all, being raised in the country *did* have advantages!

Paul knew the Girl Scouts were coming out this afternoon, and he had got home early to give Taffy an extra good grooming. Even when Nancy tried to look at Taffy through impersonal eyes, seeing her as the other girls were for the first time, she still thought Taffy the prettiest horse she had ever seen! All the girls seemed to have the same opinion. Never before had she heard so much oh-ing and ah-ing. And the mare, vain like all women, loved the attention. She took all the petting they had to give, but she reserved her nuzzles only for Nancy.

"Oh, do ride her, Nancy!" Evie begged.

Nancy looked at Grace, and at Mrs. Thomas. She wasn't sure that she ought to. It seemed selfish not to let all the girls ride Taffy if she herself rode, yet she knew the mare wasn't used to carrying anyone else. Especially now, she didn't want to excite her, or tire her.

"We know that Taffy isn't used to being ridden

by anyone else but you, Nancy," Mrs. Thomas put in kindly. "And now that she's going to have a foal, no one else should even try to. Just give us a demonstration."

So, gladly, Nancy mounted Taffy and took her out-of-doors. A path around the outside of the pasture provided a good natural ring for riding. Nancy took Taffy out to it, and let her go from one gait into the other, being careful not to let her go too fast. What she needed now was exercise, but not too much exertion.

Nancy meant to show the girls how graceful Taffy was, forgetting her own part in the show. Nevertheless she was pleased when she returned and everyone said, "Why, Nancy, that was wonderful!" and, "We didn't know you could ride like *that!*"

"You'll have to ride for Wesley in the annual Horse Show!" Evie said. She turned to her mother, "We'll tell Miss Foley, won't we?"

"Yes," Evie's mother agreed. "Nancy certainly could take a blue ribbon for the school, couldn't she?"

"What Horse Show?" Nancy asked.

"I'll tell you later!" Evie said, because Paul was coming towards them, leading his old horse, Peanuts. He wasn't a beauty like Taffy, but he was good-natured. With a shy grin, Paul said, "If any of you girls would like to ride my horse — well, go right ahead!"

The whole troop squealed with delight, and all
the girls raced to see who would ride first. Pat won.
She didn't even seem to know which side to mount
from. Nancy had thought *everyone* knew you always mounted a horse from the left. But finally,
with some help from Paul, she got on. Then it turned

out that she didn't know how to handle the reins properly. To Nancy, this was hard to believe. It seemed to her she had *always* known.

Pat started out at last, but she bounced up and down in the saddle in such a funny way that all the girls laughed. Nancy found herself laughing too but she realized she hadn't been doing it in an unkindly way. None of the girls were. They were merely enjoying something that looked funny, and there wasn't anything personal in it. When Pat came back, Nancy could see that she was laughing, too.

All the girls rode Peanuts around the track. At first Evie didn't want to. "Go ahead!" Nancy urged. "You've been on a horse before, haven't you?"

"Oh yes! At summer camp. But each time I try, it's like doing it for the first time." Evie looked right at Nancy as she admitted, "That's because I'm afraid of horses, I guess."

"*Afraid!*" This, too, was something Nancy didn't understand. Grannie and Timothy used to take her riding as soon as she could walk, and by the time she was six, she could ride nicely alone. To her, riding was as natural as breathing.

But she knew Evie wasn't joking, because when she said, "All right, I *will* ride!" she rubbed the palms of her hands together nervously. Then the girl wet her lips, squared her shoulders in the trim Girl Scout uniform, got up on Peanuts and rode away.

95

As she watched her ride around the ring and come back, her shoulders still squared, Nancy felt a great deal of admiration for Evie. And for Pat too, she admitted. It was one thing to get up on a horse and ride around before a group when you knew that riding was what you could do best. But it was something else to get on and ride when you didn't know how, and you knew you'd be laughed at — or when you were afraid.

Nancy thought of the skating experience last winter, and how she had refused to go back to the school pond until she knew how to skate because she was afraid the girls would laugh at her. Now she was ashamed. Suddenly she knew she had not been a good sport — not as good a sport as Pat and Evie and the other girls were being today. Why, no girl could be best at *everything!*

"When will Taffy have her foal?" Mrs. Thomas asked as they were paying the mare a last farewell before starting back to the city.

"About the third week in May."

"How do you know?" Pat asked in her flip manner.

"Why, because it takes a mare three hundred and forty days to be foaled, and Taffy was bred on June second."

Evie was impressed. "I suppose you wrote it down?"

Nancy couldn't help sounding important. "Oh,

yes! You've got to be careful about dates, when you're raising thoroughbreds!" She sounded so much like Grannie that Grace had to smile to herself.

Paul, who enjoyed having company, showed the Scouts over the farm before it was time to go home. They all hated to leave. Visiting a farm, especially in the springtime, was such a treat for these city-dwellers. "May we come back again sometime, Nancy?" the girls asked.

"Of course!" she promised. "Why, you'll *have* to come back, to see Taffy's foal!"

"That won't be very long," Evie said.

"No," Nancy agreed. "It won't be long, at all."

But first, there would be another trip to Kentucky, and the Derby!

9

The Kentucky Derby

NANCY'S father kept saying that he didn't think he'd be able to get away for the Derby, but Nancy had a feeling that when the time came he would change his mind. So far as she knew, he had never missed the big Kentucky race in his life. For horse-lovers, it meant a gathering of the finest horse-flesh in the country, presented under the best of conditions. In some places horse-racing seemed to be only an excuse for betting money, and in other places it seemed to be only an excuse for getting people together. But the Derby was a sportsmen's event because there in Kentucky horse-racing was still truly what it used to be called — the Sport of Kings.

Nancy was right in feeling that her father would change his mind. About a week before the Derby he received a telegram from his friend Mr. Bradford, who was Jimmy's father. He read it to her and to

Grace with a grin: "We're saving seats for the three of you in our box. Don't disappoint Jimmy, Juniper, or us."

"Well," Nancy's father said with an even broader grin after he had read it, "I guess we'll have to go. We certainly can't disappoint Juniper, can we?"

"Oh, no!" Nancy agreed. "We can't disappoint Juniper!" Then she and Grace looked at each other and burst out laughing because they knew he was really more anxious to go than anyone else. Nancy's father soon joined them in their laugh at his expense.

"Do you think there'd be room for Evie in the Bradford box, too?" Nancy asked while excited plans were being made. "I'd love to ask her."

"I don't see why not," her father said. "You children won't stay in your seats long, anyhow."

"I know *I* won't," Nancy admitted. She and Jimmy usually saw the Derby together from right up front, their heads just over the rail separating the grandstand from the race track.

"Grannie will be glad to have Evie, I'm sure. She has loads of room," Grace said.

"I'll want her to share my room, anyhow," Nancy planned. "That'll be more fun."

"Shall I call Mrs. Thomas and ask her if Evie could come along?" Grace offered.

"Please do!" Nancy begged. She trotted right along while Grace telephoned, and she jumped up and down when she could tell by the way the conversation was going that Evie could come.

It was a little hard for both girls to keep their minds on their classwork for the rest of the week, but Miss Foley was an understanding teacher. As a matter of fact she was so understanding that when she excused them from school on Friday, she told them they could make up their lessons after they got back. She knew it wouldn't be of much use to ask them to catch up on the work *before* they went away; they were much too excited! But neither did she think it would be fair to the other girls if they got away with *too* much! "I expect you to ride horseback, Evie," she said, "so that you may receive a credit for After-School Sports."

Evie groaned, but agreed. "What about Nancy?" she asked. "Does she get credit for After-School Sports, too?"

Miss Foley hid her smile. "I expect Nancy to do a lot of brushing up on her riding. We've entered her to represent Wesley in the Horse Show!"

The rest of the girls sent up a loud "Hurray!" Nancy flushed with pleasure and pride. By this time, she knew all about the Annual Children's Horse Show held by a near-by riding club. It was an important school event, and an honor to be chosen. She knew that Grannie would be pleased — this was one more thing she could look forward to telling her when she saw her!

Nancy's father decided they had better start out early Friday morning, because traffic would be very heavy later in the day. So they got off to an early start, and it was a merry ride because all four of them were in the very best of spirits. Who wouldn't be, going to the Kentucky Derby?

Grannie had their rooms ready for them, and everything was in apple-pie order. "You and Timothy must have worked like beavers when you got word we were coming!" Grace said.

"Nothing of the sort!" Grannie laughed. "I had everything ready days before I got your letter. I knew Michael wouldn't be able to keep from coming down for the Derby!"

Nancy's father kissed Grannie fondly. "Got your new hat, too, I suppose?" he teased.

"Of course!"

"Derby Day to Mother is like Easter Sunday to some folks," he explained for Grace's benefit. "She's simply got to have a fancy bonnet!"

"It's a custom," Grannie defended.

Nancy's father winked at Grace. "Personally, I think she always expects to run into some old beaus of hers!"

"*Old* beaus, indeed!" Grannie echoed.

Grannie took Evie to her heart at once. That was easy for Grannie, because her heart seemed to have room for everybody. Evie in turn adored her. She had never known a grandmother who could do all the things most grandmothers do, and some unexpected ones besides. Like riding horseback.

Nancy's father and Grace went out to dinner. The Bradfords always had a large party before Derby Day, and the party was larger this year because they were going to have a horse in the big race. Everyone seemed to think Juniper had a chance to win. The whole countryside was thrilled about it, because while Kentucky is good horse-breeding country, and the Derby is held right there in Louisville, the sad truth is that a Kentucky horse seldom wins the big event!

The first thing Nancy did was to take Evie out to the stable to meet Timothy and Blackie. Then she showed her all over the farm. It was wonderfully interesting, and Evie loved every bit of it.

"But why do they call it 'blue grass'?" Evie wondered.

"It's not really blue," Nancy told her. "It's just very green. Most grass has a lot of yellow in it, but ours is such a deep green it looks kind of blue just by comparison. It'll look even greener," she promised, "tomorrow morning when we'll ride out to The Crest!"

Evie wasn't sure she'd enjoy *going* there as much as *getting* there, because she was still a bit uneasy about horses. But she said promptly, "That will be fun!"

They might have stayed out-of-doors forever in the warm afternoon sunshine, but their stomachs sent them a little message, "I'm hungry!" So presently they went back to the house. There a surprise was waiting for them. Jimmy Bradford was sitting on the porch, grinning from ear to ear. The horse which he had ridden over was tied to the old-fashioned iron hitching-post.

"Where have you girls been?" he asked. "I've looked all over for you."

"Hello, Jimmy!" Nancy greeted warmly. "This is my friend, Evie Thomas. I told you about her."

"Sure, I know who she is," Jimmy said. "Hello, Evie."

"Hello!"

"Did Grannie ask you to dinner?" Nancy asked in a pleased voice.

"To dinner?" Jimmy repeated. "That's not the half of it! I'm going to stay here all night, too! And we'll go to the Derby together tomorrow."

Grannie put her head out the door. "I said to his mother, 'There'll be too much excitement over at your house. Better let him come here!'"

"Goody!" Nancy cried. Then she added with a

laugh, "Don't you think there'll be too much excite-ment over *here* now?"

"No," Grannie said calmly. "Because you've got to promise that when I say 'lights out,' it really will be 'lights out.' Otherwise, you'll all be too tired for the Derby tomorrow!"

"We promise!" the three children echoed solemnly.

"Why, bless you," Grannie said with a smile, "if I didn't know children, I'd really believe you! Now come on in and eat. That is, if you're hungry!"

"*If* we're hungry!" all three shouted, and raced each other through the door.

After dinner, they bedded Jimmy's horse down for the night in the stable. Then they helped Gran-nie with the dishes — even Jimmy, who tried his best even if he wasn't very good at it. When the dish-washing chore was finished, he suggested, "Let's play that game you got for Christmas, if it's still down here."

But Grannie had another idea. "I think you ought to be quiet for a spell before bedtime. I'll read to you instead."

"Oh, good!"

Nancy had taken most of her books along with her to Chicago, but there were still a few left in her bookshelf. She brought out an old favorite, and Grannie read all the parts the children liked best.

After a half hour even Nancy, who sometimes didn't like to go to bed, was nodding her head a little.

"Well, children," Grannie said gently as she closed the book, "are you ready for bed?"

"I guess so," each said, pretending, of course, that he wasn't sleepy in the least!

Evie shared Nancy's room with her as they had planned, and Jimmy took the guest room down the hall. Grannie tucked all three of them in when they were ready. "Doesn't it seem funny to you to have a boy in the house?" Nancy giggled when her turn came.

Grannie smiled and shook her head. "No, it doesn't seem funny at all." Nancy could tell by the way she said it that Grannie was remembering when her own son was little.

"Would you rather have a little boy, or a little girl, Grannie?" she asked.

Grannie had to smile again. "You won't catch me on *that* question! Besides, I couldn't say, because you see I've had them both!" She pulled down the shades, and tiptoed out of the room with another, "Good night."

"I just — love — your grandmother," Evie murmured sleepily from her side of the big bed.

"So — do — I," Nancy echoed. Her voice was even sleepier, and it trailed off into the very tiniest wisp of a whisper. She was asleep.

They greeted with joy the bright sun that shone the next morning, because it was always so much more fun when it didn't rain on Derby Day. There was time this morning for just a short ride because they wanted to get out to the race track early. They really shouldn't have ridden at all, but it wouldn't seem as if they were home in Kentucky if they didn't get up on a horse and ride into those hills around them.

Grannie decided not to come along this time because it would have meant borrowing an extra horse from the neighbors. Today even Nancy had to ride a borrowed horse. It seemed funny not to be on Taffy, although of course, even at the Stacey farm she didn't ride Taffy much any more because it was too close to her foaling time.

Grace could tell that Evie was a little uneasy about horses. "You needn't worry about the one you're on," she encouraged. "I rode that strawberry roan last time, and he was gentle as a kitten."

"Maybe," Evie admitted dubiously, "— but he's a pretty big kitten!"

They had to laugh at that, and just by laughing Evie seemed to overcome some of her anxiety. Nancy's father on Blackie, and Jimmy on his horse, and Nancy on a borrowed horse, and even Grace riding now without any fear at all, were enough to give any girl confidence. By the time they got to The Crest, Evie was no longer hugging the reins as if they were a life-belt. Nor did she look stiffly ahead of her, as if she were afraid she would fall off if she took her eyes away from the path for even a minute!

"Fine, young lady!" Nancy's father praised as he helped Evie dismount. "Give you a month here, and you'd turn out to be a fine horsewoman!"

Jimmy grabbed at the suggestion in a hurry. "*Give* her a month here!" he urged. "What about coming down in the summertime?"

"We haven't made our summer plans yet," Grace said, "but that certainly sounds like a good idea!"

"It certainly does!" Nancy exclaimed with great feeling. Why, summers in Kentucky were the nicest of all!

Evie was as impressed as everyone always was with the view from The Crest. "Only thing is," she said, "it's not like seeing it for the first time at all. Nancy has told me all about it."

Nancy's father smiled. "About The Crest, too?"

"About *everything!*"

He put an arm across Nancy's shoulders, said gently, "You do love it here, don't you?"

"Yes. But I love Chicago now, too!" she added with quick loyalty.

Then it was time to go back and get ready for the races. They all got into their best clothes, because it was like a Fair Day, and everyone wanted to look nicely dressed. Even Jimmy got out of blue jeans and into a fresh sport shirt and gabardine slacks. He looked very grown-up and Sundayish when he finally came out to join the girls on the porch.

"All set?" Nancy's father asked. "Well, let's all pile in and go."

He wasn't joking, either. They really had to pile in! He and Grannie and Grace sat up in front, and Evie and Jimmy and Nancy and Timothy sat in back. Timothy never had to be asked to come along to the Derby. He just took it for granted that he was expected to. Why, this was the biggest day of the year around Louisville!

So Timothy, freshly scrubbed and in his best clothes too, sat in back remembering all kinds of other Derbies he had gone to, and telling the children all about them. He seemed able to remember not only every horse that ran, but the time of the race as well. They tried to listen politely but they were so excited by everything going on around them that it was hard to keep their minds on what he was saying.

Soon they were part of a long, long line of cars heading for Churchill Downs, which is the name of the race track at Louisville. They moved slowly but the crowd was in a holiday mood and no one minded very much that it was taking such a long time to cover a short distance.

To Grannie and Nancy and her father even this was fun, because they seemed to know almost everyone they passed on the street or in another auto. Greetings were being exchanged right and left. Evie, who had never been in Louisville before, thought she had never visited a city that was so friendly. And Grace, who had never been to the Derby, was getting as big a thrill out of it as anyone else!

Nancy's father knew his way around Churchill Downs. He *had* to, in order to find a place to park! But he managed to find one, and he ushered his party over to the clubhouse and to the Bradford box. All except Timothy. "Nossir!" he protested, "'tain't fun to watch a horse-race sitting tight in a chair! Might as well be taking in a movie!" He excused himself, and went over to join a group of friends along the rail, old-time trainers and horse-breeders like himself.

Mr. and Mrs. Bradford and their other guests were already seated. "I thought you'd miss the first race, Jimmy," Mr. Bradford said after he had greeted everyone.

"Aw, the girls were so slow getting dressed!" Jimmy said.

Nancy and Evie exchanged a look. Actually, it was Jimmy who had taken longer to dress and to wash up thoroughly, than any of them! But they didn't give him away. After all, they knew it wasn't every day that a boy has a chance to sit in the box of a possible Derby winner, and they couldn't blame him for wanting to look his best.

But as soon as the races started, Jimmy forgot that he was all dressed up. He raced the girls down to the rail to see who would have the best position there, and from then on he jumped up and down so much that it wasn't long before his hair was back in his eyes again, and his sport shirt dirty, and his slacks crumpled. He didn't look very Sundayish any longer — but that was all right with Nancy because now he looked like Jimmy Bradford!

Each race was a treat to a lover of horses. There were so many beautiful ones that Nancy and Evie could never make up their minds which they liked best. Sometimes they picked horses that won and sometimes they didn't. But whether they won or lost they still looked beautiful when the race was over, and Nancy couldn't help wishing she owned every one of them!

Grannie seemed to feel the same way about it. Once when Nancy and Evie visited in the box, between races, Nancy heard Grannie say to Grace, "Isn't this wonderful?"

"I wouldn't have missed it for the world!" Grace exclaimed.

"There's nothing finer," Grannie said with emphasis. "All these beautiful thoroughbreds giving all they have in every race!" Then she added for her son's benefit, "And they do it only for the love of running, mind you!"

Nancy's father grinned, said to Grace, "Mother doesn't believe in betting!"

"No," Grannie replied firmly, "I'm like the horses. I'm here only for the love of running!"

"Don't let him tease you, Mother," Grace said. "I feel the same way."

"So do I!" Nancy put in.

"Now it's *three* against one!" her father cried in mock dismay.

Then it was time for the big event of the day, the Kentucky Derby itself. Now the children ran down to the rail and clung close to it. They didn't want to miss a bit of it.

Jimmy had got so thirsty with all the cheering in the first races that he had to have an ice cream cone. Now he waved it about as he pointed to the horses, naming them and their jockeys by the colors they were wearing. When he saw their own horse, Juniper, and their own jockey, he shouted so loudly that one would think Juniper had won the race already.

"Oh, isn't this exciting!" Evie murmured in that moment of tension when the horses lined up and the race was about to begin.

Nancy nodded. "It always seems as if you just can't bear another minute —" She broke off to shout as the others were shouting, "They're off!"

A roar rose up all around them — a solid wall of sound. It seemed as if an express train were rushing by very close to their ears.

Nancy and Evie didn't know it, but they were jumping up and down at the rail just as Jimmy was. In all the excitement Jimmy dropped his ice cream cone, and now he jumped down hard on top of it. His foot slipped in the squashiness and he went down. But he didn't stop yelling for even one second. He picked himself up again, still shouting, "Come on, Juniper!" and he pulled himself up to his feet and clung to the rail once more. He didn't even realize that he had fallen, and later when his mother asked him how in the world he had got ice cream all over one leg of his new slacks he had to answer truthfully that he didn't know!

Of course, the children watched only Juniper because they knew him, and to them it was as if Juniper were in the race all by himself. He had got off to a poor start and at first trailed quite far behind. But it was as if he could actually hear their shouts of "Come on, Juniper!" Little by little he crept up. Now he was bunched together with about five horses who were trailing the two who were well ahead.

"Oh, Juniper, Juniper, come *on!*" Nancy shouted as the horses thundered by again, their hoofs sending up flying bits of turf.

Now Juniper and another horse seemed to decide

to pair off together. They separated themselves from the five and pushed ahead, running neck and neck. Ahead of them was the favorite, Black Diamond, and in the lead was Georgia Tech, a horse from another famous stable.

"Come *on*, Juniper!" Evie shouted too, but if she hadn't been standing right next to her, Nancy wouldn't have recognized her voice, because it was so hoarse from all that shouting.

There was only one more lap to go. Black Diamond was pulling up on Georgia Tech, and Juniper's running mate was pulling up a bit on Juniper. The horses bunched behind were catching up, too.

"Come *on*, Juniper!" Jimmy begged. He was so excited that it sounded as if he were crying.

In a few seconds it would be over. Black Dia-

mond and Georgia Tech were fighting for the lead, and the other horses were starting to bunch up again around Juniper.

Then suddenly Juniper pulled ahead. He was really fighting with all his heart to get away from the rest of the horses. Very slowly, he managed to draw ahead of the others. They crossed the finish line, and the race was over. Georgia Tech had won, and the favorite, Black Diamond, was a close second. And right behind Black Diamond was Juniper!

"Juniper! Juniper!" Jimmy was screaming. "He showed! He showed!"

"He showed?" Evie repeated to Nancy in a puzzled voice.

"That means he pays off, if anyone was betting on him," Nancy explained. "He's one of the three winners!"

They ran back to the grandstand where everyone was congratulating Mr. Bradford. Juniper was not *the* Kentucky Derby winner, but he was a Kentucky horse and he had showed, and that meant a great deal. Mr. Bradford could have been happier only if Juniper had come in first!

"Maybe next time you'll have the winner!" somebody said.

But Mr. Bradford was still cheerful. "In the Derby, coming in third is pretty good!" he said. He hurried down to the track, to congratulate his jockey for riding a fine race — and to praise Juniper on running a fine race.

Nancy's father and the children followed him. "He's a great horse, even if he didn't come in first," Nancy's father said to her, and his face was glowing with pride and excitement. "He's got a fighting heart!"

"He certainly has!" Nancy agreed. She knew this was the best compliment her father could pay Juniper.

Timothy was waiting for them down at the track. He was grinning as happily as if he had run the race himself. One of the stable boys slapped Jimmy on the shoulder as he said, "Boy, that horse of yours sure is the berries!"

"Sure," Jimmy grinned back. "That's why we call him Juniper!"

There was still another race, but a lot of people left after the Derby. Nancy's father decided that his party had better go, too, because it had been an exciting afternoon. He didn't want Nancy and Evie to get overtired. He turned Jimmy over to his father, and farewells were made.

"You'll have to let us borrow him again sometime," Nancy's father said. "We can always use a boy."

"See you in the summer!" Jimmy called after the girls, and Nancy called back, "Yes, see you in the summer!"

It took a long time to get back to the farm, through the thick traffic. When they got there even Grannie admitted that she was tired. Grace made her sit down on the cool porch while she fixed some supper, and Nancy and Evie helped. Before it was dark, the girls were ready for bed. They were very tired, but it had been a wonderful day.

"I'll never forget it, never in all my life!" Evie murmured as she was falling asleep.

"Neither will I," said Nancy. In her mind's eye she was still seeing all those beautiful horses. And right in front was a little colt, a tiny one but as perfect as all the others. She knew that was Taffy's foal.

10

The Day that it Rained

THEY had a pleasant trip back to Chicago, and Nancy and Evie worked hard at school on Monday and Tuesday, making up for their lost day. It took all of two Discussion Periods to tell everything they had to tell. Even so, the other girls still kept asking more questions.

On Tuesday night, something unexpected happened. Mr. Stacey called. He said Taffy had come down with an attack of colic, and he had phoned the veterinarian. "Nothing to worry about," he assured Nancy's father. "Just like to keep you informed as to what's going on here."

"Thank you for calling," Nancy's father said. She could tell by his frown as he hung up the telephone that he was worried.

"Do you suppose it's serious, Daddy?" she asked.

"Mr. Stacey said it was nothing to worry about. Taffy's had these attacks on and off before, you know."

"Yes. But it's so close to her foaling —"

"Well, the vet will see her tomorrow afternoon. I'll give Mr. Stacey a ring tomorrow night, and later in the week maybe we can drive out and see the mare for ourselves."

"All right," Nancy agreed. But she had a funny tight feeling around her heart.

She was worried at school the next day, and thought she would ask Grace if she would mind driving her out. But now that she was going home in the school bus the rain was pouring down as if the sky was one giant spout, and she lost her courage.

Even though the school bus stopped right at the entrance to the apartment building in which she lived, Nancy still got wet before she could get inside. She took off her dripping scarf and wiped the rain out of her eyes. Then she stepped into the elevator, closed the door, and pressed the button marked "6." There was a whirring sound and the elevator started upward, slowly and heavily, rumbling as if it had eaten too much for dinner.

When Nancy stepped out, there was Grace standing at the open door of the apartment, waiting as she was always waiting, and just where Nancy expected her to be. "Hello, dear!" she greeted. "Have a nice day in school?"

"Oh, yes!" Nancy said, and her voice sounded absent-minded. Then she noticed that Grace had changed out of the nicely tailored clothes she wore every day to business. Instead she was wearing a pair of old slacks, and saddle shoes just like Nancy's. On the chair in the hall, she had laid out a scarf and a raincoat.

"Going out?" Nancy asked.

"*We're* going out!" Grace smiled. "I thought you might like to go out to the farm to see Taffy. Perhaps the vet is still there."

Nancy gave her a big hug. "Oh, Grace! I wanted to go so badly, but I didn't have the nerve to ask you to drive in this rain!"

"Want a snack first?"

"I'm not a bit hungry! Let's go right away!"

"Better take a handful of cookies, just in case."

Nancy slipped the cookies into her pocket, and they started out. It seemed to be raining even harder now, but the car felt warm and snug. "It's so nice of you to drive me out to the farm on a day like this!" Nancy said as they swished along the wet streets. Excited, she talked without thinking. "You know, when I first knew you, I'd never have believed you'd be so much —"

"Yes?" Grace prompted as she hesitated.

Nancy laughed a little. "Well, I meant to say 'fun,' " she admitted, "— but maybe you wouldn't like that."

"That wouldn't bother me a bit," Grace said, easily, "because you really didn't know me then."

"I *was* kind of scared of you," Nancy confessed. "You seemed so smart, and you were always so dressed up —"

Grace had to laugh out loud at that. "I suppose I did look 'dressed up.' You see, I'm what is called a 'city-child,' and I guess I dressed the part. I probably wore a hat and gloves even in Kentucky, the first time I came to see you!"

"You did," Nancy said. "I couldn't imagine you ever wearing old clothes, then — or going out in the rain like this."

"People keep changing. They *have* to, if they want to live together happily with others. That's what's nice about families."

"*I've* changed, too, haven't I? I'm not afraid to be up here, now. And of course I'm not the least bit afraid of *you*, at all."

"I should hope not!" Grace laughed.

"Of course, I love you too!" Nancy declared. "Next to Daddy and Grannie and Taffy, I love you best."

Grace laughed again, but this laugh had a different kind of a ring. "Well, it's nice to be loved, even second-best."

Again Nancy felt a little uncomfortable, as she had felt on the drive to Kentucky when she had called Grace a good stepmother. She wanted to change the subject, so she asked, "How did you ever meet Daddy, anyhow? You never told me."

"I used to know him 'way back in college."

"You did!" Nancy turned this over in her mind. "Why, then you knew him first, didn't you?"

"Before he knew your mother? Yes, I did." She added quickly, "We were only friends, however. He took me to the school proms and parties during his senior year, but that was all. Then he went home after graduating, and there he met your mother."

Nancy thought it over for a minute, and then she asked, "Grace, did you love Daddy? All the time?"

"Yes," Grace admitted, "I did but I suppose I never admitted it until he looked me up again, two years ago." She laughed a little. "Let's don't ever tell him! Let's make that a little secret between us."

"I won't tell him!" Nancy promised. She moved closer to Grace, as if sharing a secret made the physical distance between them smaller. Each day, it seemed, she felt closer to her. Why, she said to herself, sometimes it was hard to believe that Grace was her stepmother, and not her very own mother!

Paul came to the door of the barn as their car pulled up, and waved an arm in greeting. "You're just in time!" he called as they got out and ran to shelter. "The vet's still here."

"That's the man we want to see!" Grace said.

Doctor Phelps certainly seemed to know his business. He was standing at Taffy's side, completing

his examination as carefully and seriously as if she
were a human patient.

Nancy introduced herself. "I'm Nancy Irwin.
Taffy's my horse. Is she going to be all right, Doctor?"

He turned to her kindly. "That's hard to say.
She doesn't seem to be a very strong mare. All I
can figure is that she must have got hold of some
bad water. But it didn't hurt the other horses any."

Nancy nodded. "That's happened before, in Kentucky. Things seem to bother her easily. But she'll
get over this attack too, won't she?"

Doctor Phelps looked grave. "If she's had attacks like this before, it means she has a predisposition to colic. In other words, a weakness for it. She might have been born with a poor stomach — that can happen even to horses. Or she might have got hold of some kind of irritant when she was a colt, something that did lasting damage."

Nancy couldn't bring herself to ask the next question, and Grace finally asked it for her. "What about Taffy's foal, Doctor? Think there might be any trouble?"

"Can't tell until the time comes. But so far as this attack is concerned, I think she'll get over it." Again he looked at Nancy kindly, but nothing could soften the words he had to say, "But she's not a well mare, and there *may* be trouble."

Doctor Phelps left, and after a while Paul had to go on to other chores. Nancy wanted to stay longer, petting Taffy and talking to her. Grace saw that she would like to have a little time alone with her horse. "I'll go out in the car and wait," she offered.

"I won't be long," Nancy promised.

Grace ran back to the car through the storm, carrying with her the picture of Nancy's small face as she had looked at Taffy. She sat in the auto, with the rain sliding down the windows all around, and it was like sitting under a waterfall. Cut off from the world about her, she kept thinking of Nancy —

and of herself when she was a little girl. She could remember her own daydreams, and longings, and the thoughts she would never tell anyone else. She could recall the heart-hunger she felt when she seemed to be misunderstood or left out, and she knew this was a feeling all children have sometimes. And she could remember what a beloved dog had meant to her when she was a child, and so she knew how Nancy felt about Taffy.

Finally, Nancy was ready to leave. She too ran out to the car, and they started for home. They didn't talk much on the way back, but the silence was the pleasant kind that exists between two people who are at ease with each other.

Nancy's father was surprised when they told him at dinner about having gone out to the farm. "Why, it was raining cats and dogs!" he declared.

"We didn't mind," Grace said. "We were anxious about Taffy and now, having seen the vet, Nancy feels easier and so do I."

"Yes," Nancy said, "the vet thinks she'll come through this attack all right, Daddy." Her eyes met her father's across the table. "Of course," she added, "there may be trouble when the foal comes."

"Yes," he agreed, "but we're prepared for that. Aren't we?"

Again their eyes met, and held. "Yes," she repeated, and her voice didn't waver, "we're prepared for that."

"I think she *is* prepared, for whatever comes," he said to Grace later, after Nancy was in bed. "I'm proud of her!"

"So am I," Grace seconded.

"And I'm proud of you, too!" he said on second thought. "Going out to the farm in all that rain! Why, there was a time when you didn't want to step outside if there was a chance of catching one or two raindrops!"

Grace shrugged. "People change."

He closed his hand over hers for a moment, as he asked gently, "You've changed a lot on account of Nancy, haven't you?"

Grace smiled up at him. "But I wouldn't have it any other way!"

"I don't know how I'd raise her, without you."

Grace objected, "I wouldn't let you! Why, she's *my* foal!"

And in her pretty room her foal slept restlessly, dreaming of another foal. Taffy's.

II

Introducing Starbright

IT was the middle of May and Nancy didn't seem to be feeling well. She had no appetite, and no spirit. "Maybe she's coming down with something," her father said.

"The measles epidemic hit the school late this year," Grace answered, "but she says she's had the measles."

"*I* think it was chicken-pox she had. She was awfully little and she might be mistaken."

"I know. I've written Mother, to be sure. In the meantime, I'm keeping an eye on her."

But Nancy insisted she wasn't coming down with anything. "I'm just worried about Taffy," she said. "I'll be glad when the foaling is over."

"So will I!" both her father and Grace agreed, in one breath.

They had all driven out to the farm during the

week, and knew that the signs pointed to the foaling on any day. Nancy's father and Grace had hoped it would be over by the time Saturday came around. Now it was Saturday and Mr. Stacey had not yet called, as he had promised to do if anything happened. All three of them were sure that this would be the day, and they talked it over at breakfast.

"You'll come along with us to the farm, won't you, Daddy?" Nancy asked.

"I ought to go down to the office for awhile but —" He changed his mind after another look at her face. "Sure I'll come along. Just give me a few minutes to make a couple of calls."

He did his business over the telephone, and they started out. The sun was shining brightly, washing with gold the lovely May landscape. Before when they had driven out to the Stacey farm, they had delighted in picking out landmarks that showed off spring's progress. But today it was as if a veil were held before their eyes. Even a hedge of fragrant lilacs blooming along the road failed to excite Nancy, though she dearly loved lilacs.

As the car turned up the driveway to the Stacey farm and drew to a stop, there was a scene any artist would enjoy painting: trees in full leaf doing more for the outbuildings than a good paint job, grass a warm green, flowers and fragrance everywhere. But as Nancy jumped out of the car she saw the stable and nothing else, and she ran over to it as fast as she could.

She passed Doctor Phelps' car, knew that Mr. Stacey had called him. It meant the time for the foaling had surely come. Nancy burst into the barn, with her father and Grace close behind her. She blinked in the dim light, not seeing Taffy in her accustomed stall. Then she realized that the mare was lying down.

"Hello, Taffy!" Nancy cried, and went down to her knees beside her. The mare moved her head a little, and looked at her. Nancy patted her head and her neck where the golden mane lay moist and matted. Taffy's sides heaved. Nancy had seen foals born before, and she said, "She's in labor, isn't she?"

"Yes," Doctor Phelps said. "Started during the night." He turned to her father and added, "It may be quite awhile yet. Nancy ought to wait outside."

Reluctantly, Nancy turned to leave, with Grace. "I think I'll stick around in case Doctor Phelps needs a little help," her father said casually.

Nancy and Grace walked along the pleasant path that skirted the pasture. It was here Nancy had ridden Taffy on the day her Girl Scout Troop had come out for a visit. She thought of how pretty Taffy had looked that day, and how all the girls had loved her. She couldn't help wondering if she would ever ride her again, along this path or any other. Before she knew it, she was crying. She couldn't seem to stop the tears that were spilling out of her eyes and sliding down her cheeks.

Grace put her arms around her and said sympathetically, "There, there, Nancy dear!" Nancy pushed her face against Grace's shoulder and let the tears flow, and Grace patted her head and her cheek. There was a time when it would have been hard for Grace to show affection like this, because she had been brought up in a family that considered it good manners not to show one's feelings. But in the last few months Grace had learned a few things herself. Among the things she had learned was that it was no use loving someone with all your heart if you didn't let that person know of your love.

She knew that if she wanted to comfort Nancy, the best way she could do it was by showing her how much she loved her — just as she had seen Nancy show Taffy. So she held Nancy tightly in her arms and let her cry against her shoulder. Presently the child stopped crying, and said quietly, "Let's go back."

They walked back to the stable together. When they got close to it they heard a whinny — a weak kind of a whinny, but unmistakably Taffy's. They exchanged a glance, and stood there waiting as they heard Taffy whinny a few more times, first weakly, then sharply. And the last sharp whinny was answered by a funny small bleat!

Just when Nancy thought she wouldn't be able to wait a minute longer, her father looked out. He was smiling. "She's got a son!" he called.

Nancy ran on ahead and through the open door. There was a small black colt, looking wet and sticky all over, kicking its long spindly legs.

"He's black — like Blackie!" Nancy murmured. He even had a white star on his forehead, just like

Blackie's. "Isn't it a pretty star!" she exclaimed delightedly.

Grace, at the door, quoted lightly in her relief, "Starlight, Starbright — first star we see tonight!"

"Starbright!" Nancy's father repeated. "There's the name for your colt, Nancy!"

"Oh, that's perfect! Starbright!"

Taffy was struggling to her feet, instinctively anxious to nurse her foal. She seemed very weak. "Poor Taffy!" Nancy said, petting her hot flank. "But you've got a beautiful baby!"

"She'll be weak for awhile," the doctor said. "We've got to expect that — she's been a very sick mare. Yet she came through it better than I expected."

"Look!" Nancy's father burst out, "she's made it!"

Taffy was on her feet. She was wobbly, but she was standing. And the little black foal, hungry and eager, was getting his first milk.

They stayed around the farm the rest of the day, making sure Taffy was getting along well. Somehow, even at the start, no one seemed to worry about the colt. He was such a determined little fellow, one had only to look at him to feel he was always going to be all right. Nancy's father, examining him with an expert horseman's eye, commented, "Never saw a better colt!"

"He *is* nice, isn't he, Daddy?" Nancy said proudly.

"Timothy was right, after all. He *said* Taffy would have a foal like Blackie!"

Her father grinned. "Timothy is lucky!" he declared. "We'll have to send Grannie a telegram as soon as we get home." He smiled again as he thought about it. "I can see her writing it into the records now: 'Starbright, out of Taffy by Black Knight of Wales.'" Looking at his watch, he decided, "We really ought to be starting home right now. We'll hardly make it in time for dinner."

"Do you think it's safe enough to leave Taffy now?" Nancy asked.

"I imagine the worst is over," her father replied. "Even Doctor Phelps has gone. What she needs most now is lots of rest."

Nancy looked at Taffy again. She had eaten her hot mash, but she still seemed very weak. Yet this was to be expected, she told herself! After all, Taffy had never been very strong. She gave the mare a loving pat and talked to her in a low voice for a minute, then said that she was ready to go.

On the way back, Nancy was as silent as she had been on the way out, but it was a different kind of silence. Then, she had been anxious. Now she was relieved that it was over, but it was as if Taffy's ordeal had weakened her too. She felt strange, and a little ill at ease in her stomach.

When they got home, they decided they would

rather call long-distance than send a telegram. Each in turn said a few words to Grannie. First, Nancy's father, who put through the call, talked. Then Nancy came on and described Starbright. When Grace took her turn, Grannie said to her, "Well, I'm certainly glad it's over! Better put the child to bed now — she sounds sick. Too much excitement!"

"You're right!" Grace agreed. "She's going to bed right after dinner. And Mother," she remembered, "you haven't answered my letter yet! Was it chicken-pox or measles Nancy had when she was little?"

"Chicken-pox," Grannie answered. "I wrote it down. When are you all coming to visit?"

"Soon, we hope! Now that the foal is here —"

"Yes," Grannie finished for her, "maybe we can get back to normal."

They talked a while longer, and when Grace hung up she found that Nancy had already gone to her room. She followed her and found that she was lying across the bed. "Don't you want to have dinner before you rest, dear?"

"I'm not hungry."

Grace felt her forehead, and it was hot. She brought out the thermometer and found that she had a rather high temperature. "Michael," she said in a worried voice, "I think we had better put her to bed."

Nancy's father helped. They undressed her, got

133

her into pajamas, and tucked her in between the cool-feeling sheets. Grace tried to call the doctor but she couldn't reach him.

That night she kept the door of Nancy's room open, and the door of her own room, and got up several times during the night to be sure she was getting along all right. By morning Nancy not only had fever but a rash. Grace tried again to get the doctor. This time he was in, and he came right over. He didn't seem as worried as Grace and Nancy's father were.

"Has she ever had the measles?" he asked after he examined her.

"No," Grace replied.

"Well," the doctor said, "she's got them now." He told Grace what to do, and left a prescription. "I'll drop around again in the morning," he promised, "but there's nothing to worry about. She'll be all right in a week or two."

Nancy overheard his words. In a week or two! And there was Taffy needing her, and the new colt! But she felt too weak, too ill, to protest.

Towards noon, the phone rang and her father answered. "Oh, hello, Mr. Stacey," she heard him say. She could tell by his voice rather than by the words that followed, that he was very much disturbed. "All right," he said, and, "Yes, I'll tell her."

Nancy pushed her hot face into the pillow. She

knew why Mr. Stacey had called. It was news, and yet not news. This was something she had expected. This was something she had known would happen, ever since Taffy had that last sick spell. And this was why she had cried yesterday.

When her father came into the bedroom, she was ready for him. "Daddy," she asked quietly, "what did Mr. Stacey want?"

"Oh," he answered, trying very hard to sound natural, "nothing very important. I'll tell you later."

But he couldn't fool her. "Tell me now. He called about Taffy, didn't he?"

Her father sat down on her bed, and he took her hand, and he said very gently, "Yes, he did, Nannie. I'd rather not tell you now, but since you heard — Yes, Taffy's —"

"I know," Nancy said. After a minute, she spoke again. "I'm glad she saw her foal. He's such a pretty foal." She turned her face to the wall, and was so still that he wondered if she had fallen asleep.

He sat on the edge of her bed for a long time, holding her hand.

12

The Troop Adopts a Baby

WHEN the girls came to school on Monday, Nancy was not at her desk. They began to talk about it, and to wonder out loud about the reason for her absence. At nine o'clock, when classwork was about to begin, Evie said as Miss Foley came in, "Nancy isn't here! Do you suppose Taffy's foal has come?"

Miss Foley answered gravely, "I've just had a telephone call from Mrs. Irwin. Yes, Taffy's foal *has* come. But I have more news for you than that, and I'm sorry to say that all of it isn't good."

The girls sat up at attention. "Is the foal all right?" Pat asked anxiously.

"Yes, the foal is fine. It's a little black colt with a white star, and Nancy is naming it Starbright."

The girls cried out in delight. "But what about Taffy?" Evie asked. "Is *she* all right?"

"That's the sad news," Miss Foley told them

kindly. "Taffy died Saturday night. Now girls," she called out above the wails that greeted her announcement, "I know you all loved Taffy but remember that Nancy loved her most of all. And yet she is taking it very sensibly and bravely."

"Is that why she stayed home today?" one of the girls asked. "On account of Taffy?"

"No. Nancy is our latest measles victim. We had hoped the epidemic was over but now all we can hope is that she's the last to come down with it."

"Poor Nancy!" Evie said, and her voice was warm with sympathy. "She's had the news about Taffy, and she's sick with measles, all at the same time!"

"We ought to *do* something for her!" Pat said.

"Yes!" the others agreed. "Let's *do* something for Nancy."

And then somebody called out, woefully, "But what can we do?"

They all thought for a minute, and then Pat came up with a bright idea. "I know!" she cried. "What's worrying Nancy most right now, I'll bet, is the thought of that little foal out there on the farm alone, without anyone to look after it. Let's look after it ourselves! We could take turns. We could *adopt* Starbright!"

Evie, whose mother was the Girl Scout leader, instantly thought of the troop. "That's a wonderful idea!" she seconded. "Let's make it a Girl Scout project. Let's have our troop adopt that baby!"

"We can make Starbright our troop mascot!" some-one else called out.

Everyone joined in the excited discussion that followed. After a few minutes Miss Foley looked at the time and said, "Girls, I think you have a fine idea, and one which will be very helpful to Nancy. Evie, you may telephone your mother during Discussion Period, so that she can begin to get things organized. She'll have to arrange with your mothers for transportation out to the farm. In fact," Miss Foley added on second thought, "you may tell her that I'll be glad to drive this afternoon, myself."

"Oh, thank you, Miss Foley!" the girls chorused.

Miss Foley became alert again, like a teacher. "You're very welcome, girls," she said briskly. "And now we really must get on with our work."

At Discussion Period, Evie telephoned her mother, and reported back to the class. Mrs. Thomas promised full co-operation. She suggested that the girls draw lots, to see in what order they would go out to the farm each day when school was over. Evie had a suggestion to make, herself. "It was Pat's idea, so I think *she* ought to go out this afternoon, with Miss Foley. Then, starting tomorrow we can draw lots."

All the girls agreed that Pat should go out first. "I won't argue with you!" she accepted with a grin. "I can't wait to go."

Pat also had to call her mother, to tell her of the plans. "Miss Foley said she'd drop me off on the way back," she added.

"Ask Miss Foley to stay and have dinner with us," Pat's mother invited. "She hasn't done so for quite a while."

"Goodness!" Miss Foley smiled as she accepted the invitation Pat gave her. "There's all kinds of activity on account of that little foal, isn't there?"

As soon as school was out, she drove Pat over to the Stacey farm. They had a nice visit on the way over. "Why, she's *fun!*" Pat thought. Somehow in school, Miss Foley had a way of looking strict, when she really wasn't strict at all!

Paul came out to meet them at once, as he had come to meet the troop that afternoon when all the Girl Scouts paid a visit. Pat introduced him to Miss Foley. "Gosh," he said, "I guess you heard the news!"

"Oh, yes!" Pat exclaimed. "That's why we're here." In the same breath, she went on to tell him how the Girl Scouts planned to adopt the foal. "We know you'll take good care of him," she added quickly because Paul was so nice that she didn't want to hurt his feelings. "But we just felt that if we could see him for ourselves every day, and pass on reports to Nancy, she'd feel better."

"Sure," Paul agreed at once. "I think it's a swell

idea. Well, come on out to the stable and I'll show you what to do."

Pat and Miss Foley followed him. The colt greeted them with curious ears pricked, and eyes full of mischief. At once he made friends. In fact, he was so friendly that he nearly knocked Pat down by a strong nuzzle. She shrieked with delight.

"I was just going to feed him," Paul said. "My father doesn't have time. He puts up the formula, but the rest is up to me." He took up a bottle. "If one of you girls will come out every day like you say — well, that's just fine with me because it'll save me part of the job!"

Pat looked at the bottle with wide eyes. "Do you mean to say you feed Starbright a *bottle?*"

Paul had to laugh. "Sure! How else do you suppose you feed a motherless colt?" He thrust it at her. "Here!"

Pat giggled as she took the bottle. "But what do I do?"

"Just hold it out to him! He'll do the rest!"

Starbright did, too. All he had to do was to see the bottle, and he was after it. He had been trained to it since yesterday. Besides, he was a very hungry colt!

Pat decided that perhaps he was also a very greedy colt. He not only swallowed the milk in the bottle in no time at all, but he tried to swallow the bottle itself. "Goodness!" she said to him, "at the rate you're going, you'll be a great big horse in no time at all!"

"He'll be a big horse, all right," Miss Foley agreed. "You can tell by looking at his frame. See those large bones."

Pat observed Miss Foley's interest in Starbright and the other horses in the stable. On the way back to the city she said thoughtfully, "You know a lot about horses, don't you, Miss Foley? I bet you used to ride a lot, when you were young."

Miss Foley smiled. "Yes, when I was young."

Something in her voice as she repeated the words

made Pat say quickly, "I mean when you were *a girl!*" She grinned sheepishly. "You know how I blurt things out, without thinking!"

"We all blurt things out without thinking," Miss Foley agreed. With another smile, she added, "And it's usually the truth, too."

As soon as they got home, Pat called Nancy's house. Grace answered. Pat remembered her manners enough to ask first how Nancy was getting along. Then she told Grace all about the Girl Scouts "adopting" the foal, and how she had gone out that afternoon with Miss Foley. She gave a careful description of everything that had happened at the farm. She remembered to tell just exactly what Paul had said about how he had never seen such a high-spirited young colt before, and she told how Starbright was fed, and how he was thriving on the bottle.

"And one of us will go out to the farm every day," Pat concluded. "Please tell Nancy that she'll get a report about Starbright every evening at this time."

"Pat," Grace said gratefully, "I think it's wonderful of you girls to do this, and Nancy will think so, too! Please tell them so for me, and for her. You don't know how much this will mean to her!"

"Oh yes, we do!" Pat answered in her pert way. "That's why we're doing it!"

Grace had to laugh at that. She thanked Pat

again, and hung up, and went into the bedroom to tell Nancy.

Nancy, in the darkened room, listened without a word. But she laughed out loud when Grace got to the part about feeding Starbright with a bottle, and how he had gobbled up every bit of the milk, and then tried to swallow the bottle itself.

When Grace had finished, Nancy was silent for a minute. Then she said, "Isn't it wonderful of the girls to adopt Starbright, Grace? They're really taking care of him for me, aren't they?"

"Yes, that's exactly what they're doing. And you'll get a report about him every day, and you shan't have to worry about him at all!"

"I won't — now!"

And that was exactly what happened. Every day one of the girls telephoned Grace and told her all about the trip to the farm, and how Starbright was getting along, and what Paul or Mr. Stacey had to say about him. Sometimes, besides telephoning the girls dropped her a note, which Nancy could read when it came. That meant she could enjoy her "visit" all over again.

Grannie wrote often, knowing how much mail can mean when one is sick. Even Jimmy Bradford broke down and wrote to her, from the boarding school he attended. "Here's a letter from your friend, J. R.," Grace teased as she handed it over.

This time Jimmy wrote even less than he had before: *"Dear Nancy: I hear you've got a good colt, and a bad case of meazles. Glad to hear about the colt. Your freind, James Bradford, J. R."*

Again, Nancy knew that he was trying to console her by writing, this time because he had also learned she had lost Taffy.

Luckily, except for the first several days, Nancy wasn't very sick. Soon her temperature went down to normal, but she followed the doctor's advice about staying in bed for three more days. Grace was grand to her through it all, Nancy thought. As soon as she knew that Nancy had the measles, she canceled all her appointments, or put them off for two weeks. When Nancy worried about it, Grace shrugged it off with an airy, "Apartments can wait to be decorated! But measles never wait a bit!"

So instead of going down to business, Grace stayed close to Nancy's bedside. During those first days of high fever, she kept Nancy as comfortable as she could. Then when Nancy felt a little better, she helped pass the time by reading to her — any old favorite Nancy asked for, as well as the new books which her father brought to her.

Gifts from her father — like the reports from the Girl Scouts — were high-spots in the days. Whenever he came home from the office he brought her something — a book, or flowers, or little puzzles which she could play with when she wanted to have something to do with her hands. And he had a nice talk with her, every night.

"You know, Nannie," he told her gently once, "that was why I didn't want you to have Taffy in the first place. I know from experience that there's sorrow ahead for anyone who loves an animal that isn't strong and well."

"But she was so sweet, Daddy!"

"I know she was sweet. And gentle. The best thoroughbreds are high-spirited — like this little colt that's so much like Blackie!"

Nancy spoke out loud something she had been thinking there in her darkened room. "What if she hadn't had a foal, Daddy?"

He shook his head. "Taffy was never a strong, or even a very well mare. It's doubtful that she would ever have lived to the ripe old age some horses get to be." He looked out the window, and he could see Lake Michigan down below, calm in the dusk. "Remember how gray and cold-looking the Lake was when you first saw it, Nannie?"

"Yes."

"Well, now it's spring, and the lake is warming up, and all the trees are green and the flowers are blooming. It's as if everything in Nature was born over again. That's the way you've got to look upon Starbright."

"As if he were Taffy, born over again?"

"A stronger, healthier, finer Taffy."

"Yes," Nancy murmured thoughtfully, "that's right, Daddy." And she said, "I really haven't lost Taffy at all, have I? Because now I've got Starbright!"

13

Surprise!

THE three days that Nancy had to spend in bed after her temperature became normal were the hardest, because she didn't feel weak or sick any more. That meant she didn't feel like sleeping as much as she had at first, either, and yet the doctor wanted her to take a nap every afternoon.

After Grace brought lunch in to her on a tray, Nancy would lie back on her pillow and relax. Grace would lower the shades, open the windows wide, and tiptoe out. Nancy would pretend to be asleep, but she didn't sleep. She would lie there and think instead.

She would think of Taffy, but she would also think about Starbright. She would go over in her mind the reports the Girl Scouts sent her. In her mind's eye she pictured him as they described him, and there in the darkness she had to laugh to herself as she imagined him drinking his milk out of a bottle, nuzzling at the girls so hard that he knocked them over, and being high-spirited and full of mischief. All the signs pointed to his being a fine thoroughbred.

And as Nancy thought about the girls of the troop taking care of Starbright, being driven out to the farm every day by their mothers, she realized how wonderful it was of them to get together in this way. This kind of working together was something she had not known about before. She remembered how she had disliked Pat and had not cared to be friends with her. Yet when they had all gone out to the farm the first time, it was Pat who had taught her a never-to-be-forgotten lesson in good sportsmanship by getting on a horse and riding even though she knew she would be laughed at. And now she had learned that it was Pat who had first thought up the idea of adopting Starbright. It really made her feel a little ashamed.

Nancy could look back on herself now as if she had been another person. In a way, she knew she *had* been another person. She had been a little girl. Now she was beginning to grow up. It was as if she could almost feel the walls of a little girl's world spreading out. She had suffered a hard blow in losing Taffy, but she had come through it all right, and now it seemed as if new strength was coming back to her.

While she was lying there in bed thinking, Nancy

heard the door open softly. Her first thought was that it was Grace coming in to tell her that she could sit up. Then she felt a hand on her face, and she knew it was not Grace's hand. There was only one hand in all the world like this, one hand so full of loving and so used to loving that it was a little worn-out.

Nancy grabbed the hand with both of hers, and she cried, "Grannie!"

"Surprise!" Grannie said. She stooped over and kissed her.

"Watch out," Nancy warned, "you'll catch the measles!"

"Nonsense!" Grannie said. "Why, the measles wouldn't *dare!*"

She sat down in the chair next to the bed and looked at her closely. "Well, you look pretty good, at that. When you can get some sunshine and get rid of that peakedness, you'll look fine."

"I feel fine now," Nancy insisted.

Grannie smiled. "Don't try to fool *me!*"

"Grannie — you know about Taffy?"

"Yes," Grannie said briskly, "and I know about Starbright, too. For goodness sake, if that foal is half as good as your father says he is, you certainly have a fine thoroughbred!"

"He *is* wonderful, Grannie! Daddy will have to take you out to see him."

"Not until you can come along and show him to me yourself."

"Good! That means you'll have to stay awhile!"

"I intend to! You're a high-spirited little colt yourself, and Grace may need a hand with you for the next week or two."

"I certainly shall, Mother!" Grace agreed from the door.

Instantly, Nancy was making eager plans. "As soon as the doctor allows me to, we'll go out to the farm and see Starbright! And while you're here I'd love to have you meet the girls at school, and Miss Foley, and everyone!"

"That's exactly what I'm here for," Grannie said. To Grace she added with a laugh, "First you couldn't get me to come out, and now you won't be able to get me to go home."

"That will suit us just fine!" Grace said.

Getting well didn't seem such a hard job after that. With Grannie around there was always fun and excitement. *And* good food, too! Grace could cook nicely but she wasn't such an expert as Grannie. Besides, Grannie seemed to specialize in just about everything children like best to eat. She took over in the kitchen, and the whole apartment seemed to smell of good things to eat from morning until night.

Finally the day came when the doctor said he

150

thought Nancy was well enough to go out. Naturally, she wanted to go to the farm and show Grannie the colt. It was a lovely bright afternoon, and Grace drove them out.

Nancy was amazed to see how Starbright had grown. Yet he acted as if he recognized her, even though she had seen him only once. He ran right at her and butted her as if he were a goat, and then he scampered off, looking back.

"Why, he expects me to chase him!" she laughed. "I don't think he can tell the difference between me and another horse!" She turned to Grannie. "Goodness, is he *that* stupid?"

Grannie laughed in turn. "He's not stupid at all! He's just high-spirited. Come here, young fellow!"

Grannie looked him over ever so carefully, her eyes bright and shrewd. "You've got a fine colt here, Nancy," she said at last. "He's got all of Blackie's best points — and a few others besides."

"Maybe he'll be a racer, like Juniper!" Nancy said eagerly.

"We won't count on *that!* But he'll be a good thoroughbred, and that's more important."

They stayed at the farm for awhile, playing with Starbright. He was so full of mischief and so lacking in fear that Nancy could see why all the Girl Scouts had fallen in love with him at sight.

Thinking of the Girl Scouts made her realize something. Now she was well enough to be up and about again, and the girls wouldn't have to go out to the farm any more. She could imagine that they would feel a little sad about it.

"Grace," she said, "all the girls have done so much for Starbright, I'd like to feel he belongs to *them*, too. I mean I don't want them to think they won't ever get to see him again when I'm able to go out to the farm and look after him myself."

Grace had to smile. "From the excited way they talk about him, I don't think they'll let you!"

"I'd like to *do* something for them. Let's have a picnic out here at the farm for the whole troop, so that we can all have a day with Starbright together!"

"Why, what a wonderful idea! We could pack a lunch at home, and spend the whole day."

"*Pack* a lunch?" Grannie cried. "You mean *sandwiches?*" She said the word as if it was sticking in her throat just as a dry sandwich would.

"Grannie likes to cook out," Nancy explained.

"That's even better," Grace said to her, "— if you'll take over."

"Nancy will have to take over. I'm afraid I'll have to go home tomorrow."

"Already!" Grace and Nancy cried in one voice.

"I've been here a whole week."

"That's not long!" they protested.

"To a farm it is. Farms get lonesome."

In spite of her disappointment that Grannie was going home so soon, Nancy smiled at that excuse. It was a little joke in the family that Grannie never could be made to leave home, and that if she did, she could hardly wait to get back again!

She said, "I wish you could wait for the picnic, anyhow."

Grannie smiled. "This will be your chance to find out how much you've learned about cooking."

"All right!" Nancy decided eagerly. "I'll do most of it myself." She thought a minute, and then added, "If I do all of the work that I can, I'll be helping to pay the girls back, won't I?"

"You certainly will!" Grace agreed.

All the way back to town they made eager plans. They set the date for the picnic for a week from Saturday. Looking forward to it made it easier for Nancy to let Grannie go home the next day. Besides, as Grannie pointed out to her, they would see each other again in a little while. With vacation time so near, it wouldn't be long before Nancy would be making another trip to Kentucky with her father and Grace.

On Monday when she went back to school, Nancy had quite a reunion with all the girls. It took a little while for the class to come to order because they all had so much to talk about. And they all wanted to tell her again of their experiences with Starbright!

"The only bad thing about your coming back," Pat said with a grin, "is that now we can't go out to see Starbright any more!"

Now Nancy could grin too, because she understood Pat, and she knew she was only being funny. "But you *can* see Starbright, anyhow!" she answered, and then she told them about the picnic they were planning for Saturday.

"Miss Foley, will you come too?" she asked.

Miss Foley looked pleased. "Well," she said, "if you girls really want me —"

"We'd love to have you!" they cried.

"Then I'd love to come. And now I do think we really must have the class come to order!"

Evie couldn't keep from making one more remark before they quieted down. "I can't wait till Saturday!"

"Neither can we!" the others chorused.

But they had to!

14

The Picnic at the Farm

NANCY was so anxious to see what Saturday would be like that she woke up at six o'clock in the morning. She was very much relieved to find the sun already up, and she knew it would be a bright, clear day, just right for a picnic.

Nancy had also invited the mothers of the Girl Scouts, because they had been so kind about driving out to the farm. Several had accepted, so there would be plenty of cars.

By nine o'clock the line of autos was ready to start. Grace led, with Miss Foley and Nancy as her passengers. Nancy had thought she would have more fun if some of the other girls were riding along with her, but she soon realized she had been wrong. Away from the classroom Miss Foley was quite a different person. She and Grace got on well from the start and kept a lively conversation going from the time they left the city until they got out to the Stacey farm. "Why, how *nice* she is!" Nancy found herself thinking. She was glad Miss Foley was riding in their car. It gave her a chance to know her as she really was.

As the cars pulled off the main road into the driveway, the girls could see Starbright scampering about in the small corral Mr. Stacey and Paul had put up for him next to the stable. They piled out of the cars pell-mell and raced over to him.

He pretended at first that he had never seen them before in his life. Yet after they had exclaimed enough over him, pointing out to each other how much he had grown and how beautifully sleek he was, he decided to come close to the gate and sniff at them in a high-handed fashion. But when they tried to fondle him, he shied back and looked comically scornful, as if he was trying to say, "I'm a horse, not a pet!"

"He is certainly an independent little animal, isn't he?" Miss Foley said with a smile.

"Yes," Nancy agreed. "He's just like Blackie." Thoughtfully, she added, "He's probably going to be a very fine horse."

"He thinks he's a very fine horse right now," Miss Foley said with a laugh. "Look at him strut!"

He *was* strutting, showing off like a small boy before company. The girls screamed with delight. Pat called out to him, "You can't fool us, Starbright!

We knew you when you were just a baby. And if you don't mind my saying so, you were a mighty silly-looking baby!"

Starbright gave Pat a look, and it was so much Blackie's kind of a glare that Nancy laughed out loud.

"Trying to high-hat *us?*" Evie called. "Why, we fed you milk out of a bottle!"

"Oh, dear!" Miss Foley laughed. "Look at his pained expression! He looks as if he's wondering how he'll ever live that down when he's a Derby winner!"

Nancy kept looking around for Paul. She had sent him an invitation to the party too, because he had been so kind to Starbright that she wanted to do something nice for him, herself. Presently she saw him coming up the road riding his horse Peanuts. She blinked and shook her head hard, thinking she was seeing things, because it looked to her as if Paul were leading a long train of horses. There were twelve in all, the reins of one fastened to the saddle of the horse ahead.

The other girls looked around too when they saw Nancy's surprised expression. Then they cried, "Look at all the horses!" At once, they started running to meet Paul, knowing exactly what those horses were for.

Paul was not shy with the group any more because he had got acquainted when the girls had come out one at a time to take care of Starbright. As if he were a ringmaster in a circus, he rode Peanuts right in front of them, got off, and announced, "Choose your partners, girls. Compliments of Mr. Irwin."

"What a nice surprise!" Nancy said. "But where did you get them, Paul?"

He gestured over his shoulder. "At the riding academy. Your father asked me about it last time he was out and I fixed it up." He began to unfasten the reins from the saddles. "Don't be scared, girls," he said in a very grown-up voice. "They're so well saddle-broken, not one of 'em would go fast no matter how hard you tried to make him run!"

Encouraged, the girls began to choose the horses that looked best to them. Paul helped them mount. "You'll lead us, Nancy, won't you?" someone called.

Nancy looked about. There were twelve girls and — not counting Peanuts — eleven horses. She was about to make an excuse when Paul pushed something into her hands. It was Peanuts' reins.

"What about you?" she asked.

"You ride him. I can lead some of the girls around if they want me to."

Nancy thought it over. She knew this day was a red-letter one for Paul, who worked hard on the farm and never had much time for fun. "No, Paul," she declined firmly, *"you* ride him." Her excuse was a perfectly good one. "I've got to get lunch started."

So Paul got back on Peanuts and led the girls over to the pasture, and Nancy went to work. Knowing in advance what would be needed, Mr. Stacey had set out a large pile of firewood. Nancy remembered all that Grannie had told her about outdoor cooking. She soon had a nice fire going, which she built over three flat rocks so that she would have a place for the cooking utensils. Evie's mother, watching her get the fire started, said proudly, "Nancy, I wish all my Scouts could do as well!"

Another thing Nancy had learned was that it takes a long time to cook hamburgers for a crowd over a campfire — if one uses only one frying pan at a time. So she had brought along three big ones, the way Grannie always did. Then she placed four of the meat patties she and Grace had prepared at home into each big pan. Soon twelve hamburgers were sizzling in hot fat.

There was a big crock of lemonade for the children and Mr. Stacey had promised fresh milk besides. It was Grace's job to make the coffee for the mothers, and she did very well. Nancy was proud of Grace, who had never done much out-of-doors cooking, but she was taking to it like a pussy with its first saucer of milk.

The food smelled so good cooking that the girls began coming in from the pasture one by one. Nancy helped Grace lay out the paper plates and paper napkins on a large picnic table, between turning the hamburgers. They also set out a big bowl of potato chips and all kinds of crunchy relishes like celery and olives and pickles. For dessert there were chewy brownies Nancy loved so well, which she had helped Grace bake the day before . . . also, great bunches of tiny sweet green grapes that everyone always seems to enjoy.

When the first of the hamburgers were ready, they were put between buns and placed on the table along with the rest of the food. It was a case of first come, first served, but Nancy noticed that the other girls held back just as she did, until all the grown-ups had theirs first. Then there was certainly a rush for the hamburgers that were left!

Nancy was already cooking a second batch. She was prepared to serve dozens of them, and it was a good thing that she was, because they ate dozens of them!

"My, doesn't everything taste yummy?" Pat said.

"Yes," Grace put in proudly, "and Nancy did practically all of it!"

"I couldn't do any better, myself!" Evie's mother praised. Nancy was very happy that everything had turned out so well.

When everyone had finally eaten all that it was possible to eat, they sat about lazily for awhile, chatting about plans for the summer. Miss Foley made an announcement which the girls greeted with delight. She told them she was going to move up with her class, and would continue teaching the group in the sixth grade. Nancy was especially pleased, because she felt that she and Miss Foley were just beginning really to know each other, and she was sure she would be able to do better work next year than she had done this term.

"What is Nancy doing this summer?" Evie's mother asked Grace.

"She'll go to Kentucky."

"Oh, the lucky duck!" Evie cried.

Grace said to Evie's mother, "I've been wanting to call you about our plans. Mother spoke about it when she visited. She'd like to have Evie come down with Nancy."

Grace spoke in an undertone because she didn't want to be rude and talk about plans in which the rest of the girls were not included. Even so, Nancy noticed that Pat overheard. She could tell, because Pat, though she kept on smiling, pretended to be very interested in finding a four-leaf clover. Nancy remembered that whenever she felt hurt, she too pretended to be busily doing something else. She made a mental note to ask Pat to come along with Evie and her when they went to Kentucky. She knew that it would be perfectly all right with Grannie, who always said, "The more, the merrier!"

Paul had gone to do some chores — on a farm, there is always work to be done. Nancy decided it would be a good idea to help him by getting the horses back to the riding academy herself. The rest of the girls wanted to come along. Each rode a horse back to the stables, and they all walked the mile back together along the country road.

It takes a long time for twelve girls to walk a mile when there are flowers to be picked and small streams to be explored and things to be talked over. By the time they got back, the mothers said they ought to be starting for home. Of course, wails followed, but the girls finally consented to go if they could have another visit with Starbright. He was still full of mischief and very jaunty, and they carried away with them for the summer the picture of a bright young colt who had certainly left his mark upon them.

The group had to separate for the drive home. On the way back, Miss Foley said, "We have another big day next Saturday, remember — the annual Horse Show."

"Oh, yes," Nancy said politely.

"We entered you to ride, you know," Miss Foley reminded quietly.

"Yes — but that was when you thought I could ride Taffy."

"I've talked to the people at the riding club. They

said they could provide you with a very good show-horse — many of the other girls don't own their own horses, either."

"But Miss Foley!" Nancy protested, "I couldn't possibly ride another horse but Taffy!"

"I was afraid of that," Miss Foley said understandingly. "Would you rather we asked Sally Hatfield to ride for Wesley instead?"

Sally Hatfield was a sixth-grade girl who also loved horses, and rode very well. "Please do!" Nancy said.

She was quiet after they dropped off Miss Foley, and Grace was quiet. Nancy had the uncomfortable feeling that again she was not being a good sport. But, she said to herself, no one should expect her to ride another horse than Taffy in a horse show. Why, she and Taffy had been as one together, and each seemed to guess exactly what the other wanted to do. Getting on a strange horse would seem like learning to ride all over again.

"Grace," she said presently, "you think I should ride for Wesley, don't you?"

"It's up to you, dear," Grace answered gently. "If you can't, you can't."

Nancy decided, "I can't."

And the uncomfortable feeling stayed with her.

15

The Horse Show

ALL week long, that funny feeling stayed with Nancy. She felt as she had once felt at a circus, when she had eaten so much that it seemed as if she would surely pop. The difference was, this time she didn't feel as if she would pop because of too much food, but because of the emotions bottled up in her. She wanted to ride in the Horse Show — she wanted very much to win if she could for the Wesley School. Yet she had always said to herself that she could never ride another horse but Taffy, and it seemed as if she simply *could not,* even if she wanted to!

Nancy didn't say anything more about it to Grace, and she was careful not to mention it to her father, or to Evie or Pat or any of the other girls at school. It was something she had decided in her own mind, and she preferred not to talk about it. So the week passed, a week which was busy with end-of-the-term activities.

Friday when the afternoon session began after lunch, Miss Foley said, "Girls — about the Horse Show tomorrow. We'll all sit together, as usual. We'll have a chance to see some very fine horses, and some very good riding. But this year Wesley will not be represented. We just learned at lunch-time that Sally was hurt in a fall. Fortunately she was only bruised — but she was shaken up enough so that the doctor doesn't think she should ride."

A loud cry went up. "I'm sorry, too," Miss Foley went on crisply. "Whether we win or lose, it's al-ways fun to take part. But this year we'll only look on. Sally Hatfield was the only one who could have taken Nancy's place."

Nancy kept her head down. She knew what thoughts must be passing through Miss Foley's mind. She could also imagine what Evie and Pat and the other girls were thinking.

She tried to keep her mind on her work, but she couldn't do it. Finally, it seemed she simply couldn't sit there a minute longer, with that funny about-to-burst feeling inside of her. As if she moved with-out willing it, she got up from her seat and went over to Miss Foley's desk.

"Miss Foley," she heard her voice saying, "I'll

166

ride for Wesley tomorrow — if you still want me to."

Miss Foley looked at her, and Nancy saw that she had spoken just the words the teacher had hoped to hear. But Miss Foley managed to keep her voice matter-of-fact as she answered, "Good! Yes, I'm sure there's still time to re-enter you."

She waited until class was ready to be dismissed before she made the announcement to the rest of the girls. Nancy was pleased that they were all excited, but she still had doubts, anyhow. *Wanting* to do something was one thing; *being able* to do it was quite another.

It was hard for her to get any dinner down that night. Grace put a worried hand on her forehead to see if she had any temperature.

"I'm not coming down with anything," Nancy assured her. She looked from Grace to her father. "I'm going to ride in the Horse Show tomorrow, after all. Sally Hatfield was hurt in a fall."

"Good for you!" her father exclaimed. "I'll certainly be proud to phone your grandmother tomorrow night and tell her you've won a blue ribbon!"

"I'm not sure I'll win a blue ribbon or any other kind of ribbon," Nancy said in a small voice. "After all, I won't be riding Taffy."

"You can do as well on any horse."

Nancy took a deep breath. "That's just it, Daddy. Can I?"

"Why, you're a wonderful rider!" Grace put in. "Everybody says so!"

"Everyone said I was a wonderful rider on Taffy," Nancy reminded. Her eyes searched her father's again. "Taffy was a *gentle* horse. You always said so yourself. I never really handled any other, except when you or Grannie or Timothy were along." Her voice stopped, but her eyes seemed to continue talking. Her father could see the question that was in them: *Will I be as good a rider on any other horse?*

"Nancy," he said, "it's never a question of how good the horse, but how good the rider. Remember that."

"Yes," she said quietly, "I'll remember."

The next day she got into her riding clothes when it was time to go to the Horse Show. Her father called from the living room, "You'd better step on it or we'll be late."

She had to clear her throat before she could ask, "Are you coming along, Daddy?"

"You bet I am! I wouldn't miss seeing you take that blue ribbon for anything in the world!"

But what if I don't win it? Nancy asked herself. She wished for a moment that she hadn't changed her mind about riding!

The show was going to be held at a riding academy near the park. There was a big indoor ring, with a grandstand at one end where spectators could sit. Nancy saw her name posted as the entry for Wesley School on the big bulletin board near the door. She felt proud — but she would have felt a lot prouder if her knees hadn't seemed to be hollowed out at the back. It didn't help, either, to see how crowded the grandstand was.

She and Grace and her father joined the Wesley School group. Evie and Pat had saved places for them. "Aren't you excited!" Pat whispered.

"Not very," Nancy answered quite calmly. If only she were riding Taffy, and could feel confident of winning, how different everything would be! As it was, she only felt uncomfortably warm. It seemed strange to be sitting *indoors* watching a Horse Show, but this was a riding club in the heart of the city, and that was the way it had to be. Horses could be taken out and ridden in the park a few blocks away, but shows had to be held in this indoor arena.

The competition began with the smallest children first. Nancy thought they did very well, for small-fry. She could picture herself when she had first begun to ride, and she thought of how much she had learned since, and it all seemed far away. In fact, sitting here with Grace and her father watching the youngest class, she felt quite grown-up.

Finally her turn came. Her father patted her on the shoulder and Grace, who looked a little pale, managed to smile encouragement. "Good luck,

169

Nancy!" Miss Foley said warmly, and all the girls echoed her words as she marched down to the arena.

She and the other girls in her age group who were competing had to draw for horses. Except for one girl who would ride her own, all the others would ride horses who belonged to the academy. Nancy took a piece of paper out of the hat and read off the name of her horse, "Jitters." A groan rose from the stand, like smoke rising from a brush fire, and it came from the direction occupied by the Wesley School students. Nancy had not taken riding lessons here at the academy as some of the other girls had, and didn't know the horses. But that groan told her she had not made a lucky draw!

A big gelding who had not been ridden by the younger children was brought out. He was a nicely made brownish-black, the color of the gummy kind of chocolate cake. He was really a beauty, but Nancy noticed that he was also very high-strung. Just as she was thinking, "This must be 'Jitters'!" the chairman in charge of events called her name, and she knew she was right. This was her horse.

As she was mounting, Nancy saw the judges put their heads together and talk seriously for a few minutes. She could tell they were talking about her because they kept looking in her direction, and she guessed they were debating whether or not she should ride "Jitters." It was true that she looked very lit-

tle on the big gelding, but she also knew that size
didn't mean anything. It was the horse's nervous-
ness that bothered her. She could feel how he quiv-
ered from head to haunch as if electric wires were
strung in various parts of his body. It was hard
keeping him still while she waited for the starting
signal.

The judges talked to the chairman, and then the
chairman went over to talk to Nancy's father. He
only laughed and waved a hand to indicate they had
nothing to worry about. She was proud that her father had so much confidence in her riding ability
— but at that moment she wished she could share
it!

The other girls had also mounted their horses
and were waiting with her for the starting signal.
When it came, they all rode out into the ring together
and spread out in a big circle. First they walked
their horses, then they trotted, then cantered. It
looked as if Nancy were doing easily what the other
girls were doing, but as a matter of fact she was finding this much more difficult than when she had ridden Taffy. It seemed to her this was not so much
a test of skill as of courage. Above all, she didn't
want to embarrass her father and Grace, and bring
disgrace to the Wesley School. So she forced herself to swallow the fear that felt like dry cotton stuffed
in her throat, and she fought that horse every inch

of the way, feeling not so much as if she were riding but grappling with him.

Tears of annoyance stung her eyes as she came around to where her father and Grace were sitting. She refused to look at them, even out of the corner of her eye. She was too busy fighting Jitters, using her hands and her knees, using every ounce of strength in her small body. Never before had she ridden a horse like this, one that had to be coaxed to walk and forced to trot, and who fought like an enemy whenever a new order came which must be followed.

Still, she knew to her surprise that she had done well, because when the riders lined up in the center of the ring, her name was among the four called out to ride separately. As she waited her turn to go around the ring alone, she could feel how moist her hands were, and how her knees trembled from the effort she had put into pressing them against Jitters' sides. Suddenly she remembered what Grannie used to say to her, time after time, when she was first learning to ride: "Relax!" This, she said to herself, could hardly be called relaxing! How could she expect Jitters not to be nervous, when she was so nervous herself? After all, she was just as new to the horse as the horse was to her!

So Nancy *made* herself relax. She chased away all those butterflies in her stomach by reminding herself that after all, she had been riding since she was six. Why shouldn't she be able to get up on a strange horse and do as good a job as she might have done on Taffy? It wasn't the horse that did the riding — it was the person up on its back! That person was like a motor generating the power for the horse that was the machine. That's what Grannie always said, and she was right!

When Nancy was given the signal to ride alone, she took Jitters through his paces very nicely. When the order came to canter, she relaxed in the saddle so well that Jitters suddenly stopped being nervous. He spread out his huge body in a wonderfully easy stride that was like flying. Nancy rode him so gracefully that she brought an extra round of exciting applause.

But the other three finalists had ridden well, too. The judges went into a huddle, but they couldn't seem to decide which was best. Once more the four girls were called out one by one. This time a more difficult order came: "Figure-eights!" Each girl trotted her horse in a large figure-eight before the judges' stand.

Nancy was very glad the order had not come earlier in the competition. She knew that the figure-eight meant complete mastery of the horse on the part of the rider. It had to be done smoothly, with no balking. At first, when she had sat on Jitters'

back so tensely, she could not possibly have got him
to respond well. Now, she pretended that riding
a strange horse for a figure-eight was the easiest
thing in the world. She went into it without tight-
ening up, and as a result Jitters did not tighten up,
either. The merest pressure on the reins directed
the horse into the pattern he had to follow. As she
rode back to her place in the center of the ring, Nancy
couldn't help smiling a bit. She didn't think she
would take first place, but she had taught herself a

valuable lesson. She had learned that she could master a difficult horse, riding it the first time!

Most of the children who had ridden stayed at the rail instead of taking a seat in the grandstand, and Nancy joined them. Now that the excitement of competing was over, she felt a little let-down. She didn't want to go back to the others just yet, and face her father and Grace, and Miss Foley and Evie and Pat, and the group from Wesley. Most of all, Nancy wanted to be a good sport. She had agreed to ride today because she had wanted to be a good sport in the eyes of her friends — and in her own eyes as well. Now that she thought back, it seemed to her that she couldn't possibly win. The other three finalists had ridden horses which were not so difficult as Jitters, and must surely have made a better showing. Still, Nancy knew that she would not be a good sport if she went back to her family and friends and made the excuse that Jitters had been hard to ride!

Finally, the show was over and the judges began to award the ribbons. Nancy pretended to be watching the judges' stand intently when it was time to call the names of the winners in her class. She didn't want to be looking at her father or Grace, or any of her friends, and see their disappointment when the winners were announced.

The announcer's voice came over the loud-speaker:

"And now — the Annual Junior Championship Class. It gives the judges great pleasure to announce that Nancy Irwin, riding for Wesley School, has been adjudged the first-place winner."

Nancy could hardly believe her ears. *First* place? She would have been happy to have taken any of the four places! Friendly hands pushed her forward and, like a sleepwalker, she went over to the judges' stand. She didn't hear the great waves of applause that filled the arena with thunderous sound.

She had thought there would be only a blue ribbon, but the judge also handed her a beautiful trophy in the form of a small silver horse mounted on a pedestal. There was room for her name to be engraved below the inscription: "Winner, Annual Junior Championship Class."

She had to swallow twice before she could say, "Oh, thank you!"

Her words sounded so much like a gasp that the judges had to smile. One of them said warmly, "You did fine, Nancy! Jitters is a lot of horse for such a small girl!"

Then she walked back to the grandstand, and her chest hurt. All day long it seemed as if she had been holding something in. First, it was fear, then a horse, and now it was pride! She could hear the voices of Evie and Pat and Miss Foley, and she accepted their congratulations with a smile, but she didn't see them. And she could feel her father's strong hand on hers, and Grace's arm around her waist, and hear their warm words, but she didn't look at them. She didn't dare. She knew she would burst out crying if she did — and whoever heard of a girl crying because she won first place at a horse show!

The three Irwins were very much excited when they came back to the apartment and called Grannie to give her the good news. "Good!" she chuckled. "Save that blue ribbon, and that trophy, so that you can add to it in years to come." And she added what was, for Grannie, the highest compliment she could pay: "You're a good horsewoman, Nancy!"

The excitement stayed with them all through dinner when, by way of celebration, they had Nancy's favorite dessert — ice cream and chocolate sauce. But when she was helping Grace with the dishes later, Nancy became very quiet. Grace could tell something was on her mind, so she let her stay quiet until she was ready to speak. Then Nancy said:

"Grace, when we go to Kentucky after school is out, could we take Pat *and* Evie?"

"Well, we'll have to ask Grannie."

"I'm sure it will be all right with her. I — I simply can't leave Pat out! She's been such a good friend to me, and she'd be hurt if Evie and I went off without her."

"If Grannie understands that, I'm sure she'll insist that Pat come too."

"That's what I think. I'll write her tonight. I could have asked her on the telephone but I wanted to speak to you about it first."

"That was thoughtful of you, dear."

"And Grace —"

"Yes?"

"When we go to Kentucky, you know what I'd like to do?"

"What?"

"I'd like to take Starbright down to the farm. To stay, I mean."

"That sounds like a good idea," Grace said slowly.

"He really belongs in Kentucky," Nancy went on. "He's Blackie's colt too, and —" Her voice broke off as she thought of those beautiful show-horses today, kept indoors in lovely outdoor weather. No wonder Jitters was nervous! "Well," she went on, "it's not practical to keep a horse when you live in the city, is it?"

"Not very," Grace agreed quietly.

Nancy paused, trying to find the words to express herself. "I'll never worry about Starbright being away from me, the way I worried about Taffy. I love Starbright but I could never love him as I loved Taffy." She flashed a quick look at Grace. "I wouldn't want to."

Grace nodded briskly.

"Starbright doesn't *need* me."

Grace managed to get the words out so that they sounded natural even though her throat was tight: "No, he doesn't. I never saw a sturdier, more spirited colt."

She could guess what was going through Nancy's mind. Starbright didn't need her, not as Taffy had needed her. In a way, it meant her freedom for other things. It meant a happier life, not only for Nancy but all three of them.

Grace was almost right. Nancy *was* thinking of that — but more, too. She was thinking most of all of something Pat had said, in her frank way. "I just *love* your mother!" she had exclaimed. "But why do you call her Grace?"

Nancy had almost answered, "Because she's my stepmother." Even before she said the word, it sounded in her ears the way it must sound to others — the way it must surely sound to Grace. Instead she had said to Pat, lamely, "Because — I guess it's just a habit."

Now she hurried to say what was on her mind before they would go back to the living room. She spoke in the kind of shy voice she hardly ever used any more. "You know, the girls think it's funny that I call you Grace. Would you — mind — if I called you Mother?"

179

Grace stopped rinsing the plates. She didn't do, or say, anything for quite awhile. Nancy was just beginning to wonder if she had been listening when she answered in the funniest kind of a voice, "*Mind?* Why no, dear, I wouldn't mind at all!"

From the living room Nancy's father shouted in good-natured impatience, "Say, have you two deserted me?"

"We'll be there in a minute!" Grace called back.

"You get out there and talk and talk!" he complained cheerfully. "What in the world do you talk about, anyhow?"

Grace turned to Nancy, and they shared a smile. This time it was Nancy who called back, teasingly, "It's a secret!"